Bushwhacked!

Cal Sherman rolled over on the Montana sod, bullets kicking dust around him. He followed the instructions he had learned from The Manual of War; this and his experience on San Juan Hill saved his life.

He looked for Herb.

There came three deadly shots. They brought Herb momentarily upright. Herb's rifle spat once, the bullet ripping sod.

Herb went down, but Cal did not see him fall. Already Cal was on one knee, Winchester against his shoulder as he pumped lead into the buck brush behind him.

Then Cal Sherman heard a man scream.

ALSO BY LEE FLOREN

Boothill Brand
Ride the Wild Country
Guns of Montana
Callahan Rides Alone
Rolling River Range
Broomtail Basin
Broken Creek
Double Cross Ranch

THE BUSHWHACKERS

Lee Floren

LEISURE BOOKS NEW YORK CITY

A LEISURE BOOK

Published by

Dorchester Publishing Co., Inc.
6 East 39th Street
New York, NY 10016

Printed in the United States of America

THE BUSHWHACKERS

Chapter One

It was an early morning in August, 1898, that twenty-three-year old Cal Sherman accidentally saw a cold-blooded murder take place in the southern foothills of Montana's Mad Horse Basin.

Cal had spent a hot night camped in the high rimrock ten miles south of Mad Horse River. Come daybreak, he had ridden his Smoky horse down-slope to tie the big buckskin gelding in a clump of young cottonwood trees to go out on foot, .32-20 Winchester rifle in hand.

For Cal Sherman aimed to bag himself a breakfast of tender young prairie-chicken. He got no prairie-chickens, but he did see one man murder another from ambush—and to his dying day the terror of the grisly scene haunted his memory.

He had considered himself the only human in many miles until he had halted on the north rim of that clearing.

The clearing was about four hundred feet wide. Spring

rains and snow run-off water, had had grass green and high five months back, but now the drought, coupled with a boiling Montana sun, had burned the vegetation down flat and brown and ugly.

He did not blunder in on the clearing. Fortunately he checked his forward progress in time to stop unnoticed on the clearing's edge. Hurriedly, he pulled back into high buckbrush.

For out there two horsemen faced each other, twenty feet apart. Hidden in the brush, Cal Sherman gave each rider a hurried attention—and definitely did not like what he saw.

He breathed deeply. The stench of death was heavy in the air. He listened and the stink grew even stronger.

The men talked harshly. He'd not heard their voices until now because the wind had blown their words away from him.

Now he heard clearly. And what he heard was not good.

He looked at the man on the west. This man rode a sleek, blue roan gelding, half-circle V brand on the horse's close shoulder.

The man was flat-flanked, almost gaunt. Sherman judged him to be in his mid twenties, mebbeso pushing thirty. A faded blue shirt covered peaked shoulders and the rest was cowpoke clothing—black old Stetson, worn boots, Cheyenne-legged brush-cut leather chaps.

This man had his right hand resting on his holstered pistol. "We don't need you damn' hoemen on this range, Graham!" he said angrily.

Cal Sherman thought wearily, *Same old crap . . . Cowmen against homesteaders, and the cattlemen too damn' stupid to realize they can't hold land that belongs to Uncle Sam . . .*

This was none of his business. He turned to leave, then stopped—this dry brush crackled loudly under his boots. How come this pair hadn't heard his coming?

But they apparently hadn't, and that was that.

He looked at the man on the other horse. He rode an old army saddle, all buckles and rings, one of the hardest and most uncomfortable saddles a man could put his rear down on. Cal Sherman knew this . . . by experience.

Both saddles packed rifles, stocks up, in saddle holsters.

The second man was close to middle-aged, Sherman guessed. He was big and a little flabby as he sat on an old gray mare. Sherman saw white marks on the mare's shoulders.

There hair had grown in very white. Sherman knew the mare had suffered collarsores and because of this she had the white patches.

The man wore a blue jumper, old shirt, gray woolen pants, and laced boots—not cowpuncher boots. An old black hat, shapeless from use, covered his big head. He had a weather-beaten face, with rather thick lips.

The west man said shortly, "You ain't got nothin' to say, sodbuster?"

The east man said, "What is there to say? Us grangers had thet meetin' last night at Mike Western's shack. Your boss laid down the law. We talked it over after he left. I was the only one in favor of buckin' your outfit. Word of that got to you folks an' you waylaid me out here while I was lookin' for my only milk cow."

The west man said, "I believe we'll kill you, Graham."

"*We*? Who's the *we?*"

Cal Sherman knew then a killer lurked in the brush.

His blood became chilled. He hunkered even lower. Now he knew he'd make no sudden escape. To do so might bring a bullet in his back. And he wanted to keep his spine intact.

He had noticed that, while speaking, the west rider had carefully and slowly reined his bronc somewhat south, as though getting out of range if a man shot from the brush behind him.

This hidden ambusher now shot.

The bullet came from the buckbrush behind the cowpuncher. Cal did not see the ambusher. The ambusher kept himself hidden.

The rifle made a sharp *sprang*. No smoke rose over the killer's location. *Shooting that new smokeless powder,* Cal thought. *Sounded like a .30-30.*

The ambusher shot twice.

The first bullet evidently was shot too low. It hit the farmer in the guts. The farmer screamed and doubled. The second bullet took him directly in the heart.

The old gray mare leaped to one side. The farmer fell. He lay on the ground on his belly, not moving.

Then, a strange thing happened. The mare stampeded, wild-eyed, tail up—and she ran directly toward Cal Sherman's hideout.

She snorted wildly with fear. Her untrimmed big hoofs hammered the dry Montana soil. Her bridle reins dragged. She had sense enough to hold her head to one side, thus not stepping on the reins.

By now Cal was beating a hasty retreat, hoping that the noise made by the loco horse would hide his going. He wondered if the ambusher had seen him. He soon found out he had.

"Did you see what I saw, Jake?"

"See? What t'hell'd you see, Herb?"

"A man—Runnin' ahead of thet loco gray! So help me Hanner, I saw a man—runnin' there—An' he packs a rifle—"

Cal Sherman's blood turned to ice, for the crazed mare seemed to have one thought in mind, if she had a mind—and that was to run him down. She'd almost pounded over him when he hurriedly ducked to one side.

Then, the impossible took place.

The reins— The dragging long bridle reins— One whipped out and, by sheer accident, wrapped itself momentarily around the high heel of Cal Sherman's high-heeled boot.

For just the barest clock-tick, the rein tied itself around the heel—and then slid loose. But the damage had been done. The sharp forward lunge had jerked one foot under the running Cal Sherman.

Cal Sherman landed on his rump. Fear struck him. He might be dragged to death through the brush. Then, he felt the rein slip free, and he sat there, leg extended—but just for a moment.

He still had his Winchester.

A horse charged brush behind him. That would be the cowpuncher on the blue roan—the one in the clearing. Cal rolled to one side to escape the hoofs.

He heard the cowpuncher yell, "He's over here, Herb! I got the sonofabitch cornered an'—"

"Kill 'im! We cain't leave no witneses—"

The cowpuncher had his six-shooter in hand. He leaned from one stirrup as the roan thundered past. He shot down at the recumbent Cal Sherman. His bullet missed. It plowed dirt a foot from Cal Sherman who twisted his Winchester around and shot upward—and shot true and fast.

His bullet caught the cowpuncher under the jaw. It tore out his tongue and his brain and made only a small hole in his hat as it exited, for Cal shot steel-cased bullets.

The roan lunged on; the rider didn't. He landed on his head and rolled over and lay on his back and did not move.

Cal got to his boots. The deadly accuracy of his bullet had been no accident. They taught you rough-and-tumble and kill-when-you can in the cavalry. And when you put that knowledge to practice on the battlefield, it came in handy for it had undoubtedly saved his life last month on San Juan Hill.

He looked about. He was cold now, and deadly—all killer, a new cartridge in his little rifle's barrel. A small bore rifle, a .32-20. But a deadly rifle, a murderous weapon . . . in the hands of the man who knew how to use it.

The running horses had run beyond hearing-distance. For a long moment the only sound was the raucous caw of a magpie somewhere out east.

Then, "You get him, Jake?"

The voice came from the buckbrush to Cal's right. That would be Herb, of course.

Cal said, "I got him, Herb."

There was a short silence. And then, "Who is he?"

"Stranger to me," Cal said.

Then, another silence—a longer, more hanging silence. And Cal Sherman knew his bluff had not worked. Herb knew that Jake had not spoken, Sherman felt sure.

Accordingly, he made his plans.

Herb would come on foot. He'd not ride in. By riding in, he'd make a lot of noise,and noise was something the killer couldn't afford. Not right now, anyway.

Later on in some saloon, maybe—boasting how he'd gunned down a man out in the brush, and killed him? . . . Cal Sherman's face had lost its boyishness; it was hard and slanting, his lips tight, the blue-gray eyes narrowed and thoughtful—and yet, deep inside, a faint sort of sorrow.

He'd killed once this glorious Montana morning. He had rolled out of his blanket, there on the rimrock, and the beauty of this virgin land had been on him—Montana with its snow-tipped mountains, its broad fertile valleys and rolling cut-couless.

He knew he'd have to kill again. Or he'd be killed. It was that elemental, that simple. And he didn't want to be killed. Nor did he want to kill. But before he'd be killed, he'd kill again.

He used all the jungle-savvy he'd learned in training camp and his few days in the stinking, torrid Cuba brush. And because of this knowledge, he soon stalked this stranger known only as Herb instead of his being stalked by Herb.

He gave his predicament momentary but deep thought. Herb had seen him in the brush. That meant Herb would recognize him again when and if he again saw him.

For a moment, he looked north.

North stretched Mad Horse Basin. Twenty odd miles wide north and south, he figured, and fifty or so east and west. The beauty of the wilderness scene struck him and he thought, *No wonder the redskin fought to hold it. If I were an Indian, and they tried to take it from me—I'd die first, but only after I got me a Custer or two to take along on that long ride to the Happy Hunting Ground. . . .*

He saw a small town situated in the timber along what he guessed was Mad Horse River. It looked calm and peaceful in the hazy distance. He wondered about the people the town held.

He judged them to be good and honest people. It seemed impossible that in such a pastoral scene there could be evil, but apparently there was—for did not a stranger search this brush with a weapon to kill him?

Had he not just killed a man?

Did not a dead man lie, back in the clearing?

He decided, then and there, that if the chance came, he would kill this man named Herb, for had not Herb just cold-blooded shot a man through the heart? And from ambush, also?

And what is lower than an ambush killer, Cal Sherman thought. And, ten minutes later, he killed Herb Snodgrass.

He had narrowly missed being killed by Herb Snodgrass. Common sense dictated that Cal Sherman work his way toward his big buckskin, for a man in a situation as dangerous as this needs must have an escape-exit for security.

He put himself in the killer's boots and thought from the murderer's point of view.

Herb had just cold-bloodedly murdered another human. A stranger had seen him commit the ambush killing.

If that stranger were allowed to live he might report this crime to legal authorities. He might be arrested. This stranger would testify against him. This testimony could lead him up the thirteen steps to the gallows.

This stranger would have to be killed.

Cal Sherman had not seen Herb. The ambusher had been hidden when he'd murdered the farmer. Still, that cut no ice. Herb did not know that Cal had not seen him.

He didn't know that Cal wouldn't know him if he met him on the street in Mad Horse town. He had no way of knowing that Cal had not seen him. It made no nevermind either way.

Cal *might* have seen him. Cal *might not* have seen him. But either way, to make sure, Herb had to kill Cal Sherman.

When you killed from the brush, you coppered all your bets. You left no possibilities open.

Herb would naturally figure the stranger had a horse nearby. Men didn't go wandering around this wilderness during this terrible heat on foot. This was miles and miles from nowhere.

Common sense told Cal Sherman that Herb would get on a high point and search the rugged terrain for the stranger's saddle-horse. He'd left the buckskin on picket in a clearing below. Herb couldn't miss spotting Smoky.

Therefore Cal decided to work down-slope to his horse. Herb should soon be staked out somewhere in Smoky's vicinity, Cal figured.

Slowly and carefully, Cal worked his way down-slope, moving from this boulder to that, utilizing every protection offered. Finally, he came to Smoky.

He squatted, rifle across his knees, looking this way, then that, adding facts, coming to but one conclusion.

Herb had reached the horse. Herb was in the brush down-hill, hidden and waiting to kill. How did Cal know?

Smoky told him. Smoky should have been head down, grazing. Cal had watered him that morning at a rimrock spring. Smoky had a bellyful of water. And now he should have been grazing.

But Smoky wasn't. Ears pricked, Smoky looked at the brush to the north. Something there interested Smoky. Cal knew what it was, too.

You didn't play it wise, Herb boy.

You got below the horse. The wind brought your stink to him. You need some war training, Herbie . . .

Cal Sherman decided to come in behind Herb. Accordingly, he worked his way west, circling Smoky.

He took his time. He used precautions. The sun climbed higher. The sun gained heat.

Sweat formed under Cal's flat-brimmed black hat. His shirt clung to his back. He paid these facts no attention. When your life is in peril sweat means nothing.

He kept Smoky in view. He'd raised Smoky as a colt, down in Arizona Territory. He'd found the small colt in a dying condition. Apaches had killed Smoky's mother for the *olla*. They'd left Smoky behind to die. Cal had bottle-fed the colt. Nobody was taking Smoky from him. . . .

Then, he saw Herb.

Herb sat in the shade of a sandstone boulder. He held his rifle. He was around thirty, squat, hard-looking with a peaked, narrow face. Cal watched him for a long moment, judging the man.

Then Cal Sherman said, "You'll have to kill me to get that horse, you bushwhacking sonofabitch!"

Cal Sherman's words smashed across the brush. He expected Herb to suddenly leap upright, face torn by surprise—but this Herb did not do.

Herb merely looked at him, then at his .32-20. "You saw me kill that damned farmer?" Herb quietly asked.

Cal Sherman was puzzled. Herb wasn't following the

right pattern. Something was wrong, here—drastically wrong. . . .

Then, Cal understood. And he momentarily cursed himself for being a stupid fool. For he should have scouted deeper into the buckbrush. Herb's calmness told him that Herb had a rifle staked out behind him.

Cal's breath froze. Then from behind came a harsh, masculine voice. "I've got my rifle on his spine, Herb boy!"

"Kill the sonofabitch," Herb ordered.

Chapter Two

Cal Sherman hit the ground. And he rolled over three times, a bullet kicking up dirt beside him. He followed the instructions of the Manual of War.

He'd used the same maneuver only last month. It had then saved his life. It now did the same.

For out of his rolling came two fast, deadly shots. The brought Herb upright momentarily. Herb's rifle fired out but already dying fingers were pointing the rifle down, not level.

Herb's bullet tore soil at Herb's boots. Herb went down, but Cal did not seem him—for Cal was on one knee, Winchester raised, and he pumped lead into the brush behind him.

A bullet smashed into the bole of a nearby small cottonwood. Flame lanced from the buckbrush a hundred feet south. The flame told him where his enemy was located.

Although he fired rapidly, he fired accurately. Hours

spent with the Rough Riders on the Arizona rifle-range paid off.

He heard a man scream. He kept on firing until his hammer clicked on an empty chamber. Then he rolled again, this time into some brush, and he lay there on his belly, hand digging into his pocket for extra cartridges.

His fingers trembled as he reloaded.

He listened. He heard only Smoky's snorting. He heard no retreating boots, no fast-running hoofs.

But training told him not to go directly to the hidden gunman. The man might be playing sleeping-opposum. He'd seen that happen at the base of San Juan Hill in Cuba last month.

The Spaniard had lain as though dead. A Rough Rider had walked up on him. The Spaniard had suddenly come alive. The Rough Rider had suddenly become dead.

He looked at Herb.

Herb lay on his belly. He had his nose in dust. Common logic told Cal a man couldn't breath with his nose buried. And if you don't breath, you're dead.

Cal Sherman breathed deeply. Luck had been on his side, for once. Yes, and hard, intensive training. Captain Bucky O'Neill had drilled his Rough Riders hard and accurately back on that Prescott training ground.

Damn it, and good old Bucky had got his—right through the throat—on San Juan Hill. . . .

These thoughts were out of place, and Cal Sherman knew that—but the past lives with a man, even if he doesn't want it.

Herb's dead. That other sonofabitch, though— I'd better do a little scouting. . . .

Twenty some minutes later, he'd located the man. He was short and squat and he lay with his rifle beside him, face pointing upward at the blazing sun.

Cal remembered reading that if a human eye looked unblinkingly at the naked sun but for a few moments the human eye would be burned out and forever useless. This man stared with open eyes at the Montana sun.

But he didn't see it. Therefore he had no pupils to burn out. And if they did burn, he'd never know it.

He was as dead as dead could ever be.

Cal Sherman sat with his back to a stunted box elder tree and looked at the dead man. Four men had been killed within less than an hour and he had killed three.

God almighty, such a beautiful morning, and what a hell of a thing to spoil it like this!

Cal Sherman sat. Cal listened. Cal caught his nerves, settled them, again became Cal Sherman—he was tall, he was young, he was deadly.

He heard only a meadowlark singing somewhere beyond the clearing in which Smoky grazed. He looked out over Mad Horse Basin.

He'd never seen Mad Horse Basin before. He had seen the wilderness of Arizona Territory, of the Territory of New Mexico. He had sat on a hill and looked at the endless sweep of Texas.

Miles after miles of brush, of *cholla,* of *mesquite.* Blue skies broken only by fragments of clouds, lazy and sleepy and hanging from the sky with invisible strings.

But never had his blues eyes seen such a beautiful scene as Mad Horse Basin.

Across the Basin rose the pointed horns of the Highwood Mountains, the taller peaks still sporting snow. He knew they were called the Highwoods for back in Billings—down on the Yellowstone—he'd bought a map of Montana, and that map had labeled these northern mountains the Highwoods.

West were other snow-tipped peaks. East the land ran out and became badlands and become lost to the eye.

He added up points.

Somebody had sent three gunmen out to kill a man named Graham, evidently a homesteader. He'd walked accidentally onto the bushwhack-killing of Graham and in return had had to kill the three who'd set out to kill Graham.

Was there more than three?

He discarded this thought. Had there been another the firing would have attracted him and by this time he'd have made his presence known.

Cal Sherman worked his way to the third man he'd killed. The man's wallet contained two gold double-eagles—forty dollars—and a few silver coins. A folded letter there identified the man as Wilford Martin. The address was Mad Horse, Montana and the return address was worn thin and could not be read.

He restored the old wallet to Martin's hind pocket after taking from it the two double-eagles. He then searched Herb's pockets. Herb's wallet also had two double golden eagles.

He kept those, too.

He then searched Jake's pockets. Herb had no identification; neither did Jake's body, but Jake's worn old wallet sported two gold double eagles, also.

Cal restored Jake's wallet. He then stood and looked at six shiny gold eagles made by Uncle Sam in Denver, Colorado.

The setup was crystal clear. Somebody had apparently paid each of these of these dead men two gold double eagles to kill the farmer named Graham.

He looked across the clearing at the dead farmer. The thought came that perhaps Graham left a wife and children behind. Cal Sherman put the one-hundred and twenty-bucks in gold in his pocket, grinning satanically.

Herb, Jake and Wilford Martin were where money didn't count. Sooner or later they'd be missed and somebody would ride out looking for them. When found, their pockets would be searched, and somebody would undoubtedly steal the money.

You didn't bury dead men with full wallets.

He'd not keep the money for himself. He still had most his army severance pay. He'd find some way to use it for the greatest good. Maybe, in some way, he could get it into the pockets of the Graham family—that is, if there was such.

Two hours later he discovered that Graham had at least one child, and she was one of the most beautiful and healthy young women he'd seen in his short lifetime—even counting those small, dark-eyed, well-developed Cuban *senoritas*.

By then Smoky was hidden in a deep canyon a mile north. Field-glasses under his gun-belt, rifle in hand, he'd come back on foot to the kill-scene.

He'd carefully scouted a fast exit, if one were needed. He'd merely drop down into the canyon and scoot.

His field-glasses picked up the daughter as she slowly rode toward him along the rim of the foothills.

Cal remembered the dead farmer saying he'd been looking for a strayed milk cow—his only cow.

He guessed that the three killers had run the cow off in the night knowing that come daylight Graham would ride out looking for the missing critter—and ride into their deadly bushwhack-trap.

The girl rode back and forth, plainly searching for the cow—or her father. She looked into brush clumps and, all the time, she rode higher and higher, carefully scouting the territory.

Finally, she rode into the clearing.

She was about a hundred feet away. Cal Sherman lay behind boulders, covertly watching.

She suddenly pulled in her old horse. She stared at the dead man for a long, horror-filled moment, mouth open, eyes apparently not believing what they saw, a terrified look on her young face.

She dismounted. She ran to the dead man. She cried, "Daddy, Daddy! What happened, Papa?"

She then realized her father was dead. Cal saw her put her red curls against her father's face. She began to weep.

Cal's heart went out to her. He remembered the gold pieces. Then he realized money could never ease the pain in her heart. He decided to remain hidden. It was better, that way. . . .

"Poor Mama! This will kill her, Daddy! She loved you so much—So did Bill, and me—That sonofabitch of a Mel Powers—He sent men out to kill you, Daddy!"

She wore tight levis. Her blue shirt peaked upward womanly-proud. Cal judged her around twenty, give or take a year or two. She was all woman, all beautiful.

She raised her red head. She looked carefully about. Her eyes searched the surrounding buckbrush. For a long moment she looked Cal Sherman's direction.

Cal knew she could not see him because of the brush. He lay very still and unmoving. Finally her eyes moved on.

Cal silently and discreetly withdrew.

An hour later, he was in the pass leading south to the Bull Mountains and the Yellowstone, retracing his path. He rode Smoky across a sandy bottom, then dismounted, carefully studying the imprint of the horse's shoes.

Smoky was shod only on the front hoofs. He got the

horse's shoes changed back in Billings. Smoky had been shod on all four in typical cavalry-horse, United States Army style.

The shoes had had toe-cleats. Cal had had all four Army shoes pulled and running-shoes nailed on only the buckskin's forefeet.

The shoes now left no tell-tale points that could identify the horse later on. The shoes made mere quarter circles, no more.

Hundreds of horses around this point wore similar shoes, Cal reasoned. He swung up and rode south. Once out of the rough country he swung west, riding toward the Big Dog Mountains that made up Mad Horse Basin's wetern flank.

He'd changed his plans. He'd intended to ride directly into Mad Horse town, but not since these killings. Any stranger riding anywhere on this range would now be suspect, he figured.

From the southern hills he'd noticed a series of high buttes directly west of Mad Horse town and on the north bank of Mad Horse River. They were scattered out at least five miles apart. They were lonely sentinels in this lonely northern land.

He'd climb the highest butte. From there he could watch proceedings on this prairie below, field-glasses making close inspection.

He judged the distance to be ten miles or more to the butte he had picked out—a flat-topped mesa slightly higher than the others with Mad Horse River running close to its southern base and Mad Horse town some three miles or so to its east.

He took his time, carefully watching ahead and to all sides and his backtrail. Occasionally he caught glimpses of the basin below.

He counted a dozen or so small shacks below which evidently were homestead buildings. Each had a brush barn or some such shelter for animals. The houses were mere *jacales* usually made of logs or rough lumber. A few head of cows were nearby.

He put his field-glasses on one such. A woman was in the yard throwing grain to chickens. Two children played in the shade of a shed.

These evidently were the farmers Jake Hersey had mentioned while arguing with farmer Si Graham. Cal Sherman noticed barbwire fences running down-slope to the north.

A few of these fences enclosed green fields. He judged these to be alfalfa or some other hay because at this time of the year wheat and head-crops would be brown and ready to harvest, not green and glistening under the hot sun.

He wondered how forage plants could be so green. The native grass was burned brown and short from lack of rain. Back in Billings he'd heard that this country had had no rain for weeks and cattle were getting thin when, at this time of the year, they should have been fattening for fall-shipments east to slaughter-houses.

He soon discovered why the green brightness. Back south behind two of the shacks he saw sunlight glisten on water. This water was held in coulees behind rock and earth dams.

These fields had been irrigated. The farmers had used their heads. They'd constructed these dams and imprisoned what little rain there had been. This they had turned downward through ditches to their fields.

He reasoned that these farmers had been on this range for some months for you didn't build dams and impound water within a few days. Nor did alfalfa or any other forage grass immediately sprout and cover the ground within a few months.

He put his field-glasses west. Mad Horse River came out of the Big Dome Mountains through a deep and narrow defile cut by centuries of water flowing over Montana granite.

Where the angry river erupted onto the plain would be an ideal spot for a high dam, Cal knew. He'd seen such down on his home-range in Arizona Territory.

Once water had hit the Arizona desert, the sands had produced crops within a short time, changing the brownness to a sea of productive green. The same could be done here on Mad Horse Basin, that defile told him.

These farmers were irrigating only a scant rim of the basin. With a big dam, and hundreds of thousands of cubic feet of water impounded behind it—

A grim elation touched him, driving away the bitter taste of this day's grim deaths. Already he'd rationalized. Jake Hersey, Wilford Martin and Herb Snodgrass had had but one thought in mind—to kill him.

By mere fortune, he'd killed them instead.

He'd searched long miles for a valley like Mad Horse Basin. He hoped the end of the trail was at hand. He was tired of range-bumming. Time a man settled down—

He put his attention again on the range below. Riders moved across it like black ants against brown and rough canvas. He remembered the anguished cries of Si Graham's daughter upon finding her father's body and her mentioning the name Bill. He'd at that time figured Bill was her brother.

Bill had evidently been out looking for his father also for from the rimrock Cal had seen the daughter climb a high rock and stand and waved a white cloth, evidently a handkerchief.

This had brought in a rider. Cal's glasses showed him to be a young man. The man knelt beside the dead man and then rode hurriedly downslope toward Mad Horse town, leaving the daughter behind with the corpse.

Cal knew Mad Horse town was a county-seat. His map had shown him that. That meant then that the county court-house—and county officials—were in the town.

The sheriff and deputies would be there.

By the time Cal Sherman had reached the western end of his circle riders were streaking out of Mad Horse town heading for the murder scene. Cal hunkered on a high ridge and watched through his field-glasses.

He remembered the girl mentioning the name of Mel Powers. He'd added two and two and hadn't got five.

Jake Hersey had accused Graham of being a sod-buster. Hersey, Martin and Snodgrass had evidently been sent by a cowman to kill Graham. Cal figured that cowman was named Mel Powers.

His glasses searched Mad Horse Basin for the many buildings of a cow-outfit. He was surprised to find none. Outside of the town, the only buildings he could see on this vast range were those of the farmers hugging the southern foothills, each settled below a coulee, each coulee holding impounded water.

He scowled. Some points here didn't add up. He surrended himself and thoughts to the passage of time, figuring that in time he'd have the answers, for he intended to look over Mad Horse town and this range carefully—judging and exploring them both to great lengths as to people and circumstances.

Riders scurried this way, then that. He saw two ride up Midnight Pass eyes searching the dry soil, bent in saddle. He had no fear they'd pick up Smoky's tracks.

A wagon road ran through Midnight Pass. Many

horse-hoofs shown there. Nothing special about Smoky's shoes would give any tracker a clue.

A wagon came out from town. The bodies were loaded in this. The wagon and its grisly burden then turned north, leaving riders behind searching for tracks.

Cal Sherman grinned ironically. These riders below were mystified. Four dead men, and how come all four were killed—and who killed which one? Mad Horse range had plenty to talk about.

He did not ride down and across the valley to the high butte until night fell. Stars danced in the blue dome but there was no moon. He watered Smoky at the butte's foot and then climbed it on foot, leading the buckskin.

He spent three days there among the huge boulders.

Chapter Three

Mad Horse town was in a ferment. Four bodies had been discovered in the southern foothills of Mad Horse Basin.

One corpse was that of the farmer, Si Graham. His son, Bill, had brought the news into town. The other three belonged to Half Circle V hands, namely Wilford Martin, Jake Hersey and Herb Snodgrass.

That same afternoon Half Circle V's young owner stood on the porch of Mad Horse's only saloon, the Mad Horse Hotel and Bar, owned by one Mickie O'Hannigan, who had come into Mad Horse Basin years before when old Warren Powers, the man who had built Mad Horse town, had trailed in Texas longhorn cattle.

But now old Warren Powers slept the never-ending sleep under Montana's alkali sod, having been lowered into his grave last October when a bronc had slipped on the ice, rolled over twice on the old cowpuncher, and crushed him to death.

Now old Warren's only get—Mel Powers—watched Mad Horse riders come and go.

Mel Powers was dressed from boot to head in pure, glistening white. White Tom Watson Stetson, white silk shirt, white suit even to buttoned vest, despite the rolling heat encasing the rangelands.

A broad white calfskin gunbelt, loaded with heavy .45 cartridges, hugged his hips, two white calfskin holsters tied to his thighs with white cord.

On each side stood his two gundogs.

These two, squat men were a few years older than young Mel Powers. They were twins who had ridden in last Christmas in response to an ad Mel Powers had run in the Billings *Gazette*.

They given their names as Max and Ted, neglecting to add their surnames. They'd easily passed the test their soon-to-be boss had given them.

The first shooting-test was the old can test. You threw up a tin can and the other guy drew and fired. Each hit the can six times in succession, emptying their shortguns.

Both successfully passed the *jackrabbit* test. That test required a man on a green bronc that wanted to buck chasing a jackrabbit which dodged and twisted through high sagebrush at least twenty yards ahead.

Each had killed his jackrabbit with one shot each, both shooting the hare through the head.

They'd also passed other tests of shooting ability. Mel Powers had hired them saying, "How the hell can I tell which is Max and which is Ted?"

For they were identical twins. They parted their hair in the same manner. Their faces were identical. No mole, no scar, nothing identified Max from Ted. Now one of them grinned.

"You never will be able to tell which is which. Even

our dead mother couldn't tell us one from the other." They were both the same height and build.

"Teachers in school couldn't either," the other informed.

"Didn't know you'd ever gone to school," Mel Powers had sarcastically said.

Neither twin had answered. Plainly, they didn't like this overbearing, tall, sarcastic man dressed in shining white. Both considered him a dude cowman, a show-off—but money was money and they needed the good wages he had offered.

Mel Powers had figured both as maybe wanted in Texas. He'd discreetly gone over their seemingly unbranded horses while they'd been in his barn. The horses packed no visible brand.

But on the left side of each's neck, high up and under the mane, he'd discovered a small X burned into their glossy hides.

His father had told him about Texas' X outfit. They branded good horses under their manes in order to escape marring the bronc's hide.

Mel Powers had judged these horses as stolen horses. That meant these two were under the shadow of a hangman's noose, for they hung horsethieves down in the Lone Star State, his father had told him.

Four years ago—when Mel Powers had been nineteen—he'd hand-whipped his father and pulled out.

"Have to do something about identifying you two," he told Max and Ted. "I want to know who I'm talking to when I talk."

"How you gonna do that?" one asked.

"You'll find out soon enough."

"There's a lot about you I don't like," one gunman had said.

Mel Powers had turned pale blue eyes on him.

"There's a lot about me I myself don't like."

Ted and Max let that ride. They judged this young cowman as a vain and ignorant fool. Mel Powers changed their minds—and rapidly changed them—next day down in Mad Horse town.

It was the week of Christmas. Snow was deep and blizzard after blizzard had raged. Half Circle V cattle were dying by the dozen out on the below-zero ranges.

This didn't seem to bother young Mel Powers a bit. He'd been on this range only a month or so, coming in when he'd got word—wherever he'd been—that his father had been killed and he had inherited huge Half Circle V and its herds which ran into thousands of head.

He was old Powers' only heir. His mother had died giving him birth. The Old Man had raised him.

And that Christmas Day young Mel Powers had looked at Max and Ted and had said, "Now comes the time to establish an identification mark."

"How you gonna do it?" one twin asked.

"With a six-shooter," Mel Powers said.

Max and Ted exchanged amused glances. What was this white-gowned punk talking about, anyway? He was just a dude, nothing more.

No dude could sling a gun. Mel was just a fraud, no more—sporting two guns, and undoubtedly an amateur with either.

"Which one of you wants to be changed?" Mel Powers asked.

Neither twin spoke. They didn't know what was ahead and he apparently wouldn't tell them. Or would he?

"What's the test?" one twin finally asked.

"We get back to back out there in the street with the whole town watching. We walk out fifty paces each, then on a command from the sheriff we turn and fire."

"You must want to commit suicide," one twin said.

Neither knew that Mel Powers had spent the last three years riding with Buffalo Bill's Wild West Show. He'd been Buffalo Bill's crack pistol and rifle shot.

He'd matched guns with the fast-gun, Annie Oakley. He'd beaten Annie to the draw and hit the target nine times out of ten but it had been secret for the Big Money was booming Annie, not Mel Powers.

He'd played the circuit under the assumed name of Blade Hamilton. Therefore apparently nobody in this area knew of his power with either a rifle or a shortgun.

"One of us will kill you," one twin said and grinningly added, "Then who'll pay us wages?"

"None of us will die," Mel Power assured.

The twins then drew lots. The one with the longest slip of paper would face the Half Circle V's owner. Sheriff Ike Monday held the slips. One naturally pulled the wrong slip and he and Mel Powers stalked out onto the hoof-packed snow with the twin grinning satanically and Mel Powers' boyish face bland and without a trace of emotion.

The thermometer read twelve below zero. There was, for a chance, no wind. Powers and the twins shed their sheepskin overcoats. Each wore angora chaps and overshoes.

Mel Powers' chaps and overshoes were white, as was his shirt and hat and bandana tied over his ears to keep them from freezing. The twin was dressed in coal-black as his boss had ordered.

Powers had mailed away for the coal-black outfits. The twins didn't know where back East he'd ordered them but they'd finally come in time.

The twin and Powers stood back to back. All of Half

Circle V and the entire Mad Horse range was on hand to witness, lined up in sheepskin coats and standing on the snow-covered plank sidewalks in front of the saloon.

Onlookers held their breaths. They were seeing what some considered the most foolish thing that had happened in Mad Horse town, and Mad Horse town had seen some awful foolish things in its short existence.

Two apparently sane men were apparently trying to kill the other, and for no apparent reason. They'd not quarreled. They had no hard feelings between them. They had no reason to be out there pacing away from each other with Sheriff Ike Monday slowly tolling numbers.

The sheriff reached fifty. Both contestants stopped, backs still to each other. Monday wet his lips. "You two aim to go through with this foolishness?"

"I do." This from Mel Powers.

"How about you, Twin?"

"He wants guns. I go with him."

Monday said carefully, "I'll count to five. On five, turn and fire, you goddamned idiots."

He began slowly counting.

At five, the two gunmen turned, guns leaping from leather. To the surprise of the onlookers Mel Powers' gun exploded a full clock-tick ahead of the twin's roaring .45.

The twin's bullet missed. Suddenly, the twin reeled to his right. He dropped his smoking short-gun and grabbed for his left ear.

Blood showed around his left ear. Onlookers had at first thought he'd stopped a bullet in the body. They now understood.

Mel Powers had shot off the twin's ear-lobe.

Mad Horse watched in awe. Never before had its

citizens seen such fast and sure shooting.

"Earmarked the bastard for life," a townsman later said to his nagging wife. "Too bad both of the sonsofbitches didn't kill each other!"

"Don't let Mel Powers hear you say that!"

"I suppose you'll tell the bastard?"

"I might, at that."

"Happily married couple," the man told the world.

Mel Powers had reloaded, grinning widely. Sheriff Ike Monday waddled out and picked up the fallen pistol while fat Doc Watson looked at the torn ear.

The twin stood, face as white as new snow, trembling.

"I didn't even see your hand move," he told Mel Powers.

Mel Powers holstered his gun. "The hand is quicker than the eye," he informed. "Which one are you?"

"I'm Max."

"I'll know you by your earmark." Mel Powers turned and looked at Ted who finally had clamped shut his gaping mouth. "You want me to earmark you, Ted? If you do, come out and come back to back with me. I'll take the right ear on you, though."

"No thanks," Ted hurriedly assured.

Max said, "Come along, everybody. Drinks are on Half Circle V."

Now Mel Powers stood with his two gunmen and watched a wagon lumbering by that carried the corpses of Graham, Snodgrass, Hersey and Martin, each corpse fresh and gory.

And Mel Powers was completely mystified.

This morning he'd sent Snodgrass, Hersey and Martin out to chase Si Graham's only milk-cow out into the brush. Graham had advocated riding out with rifles against Half Circle V last night when the grangers had met at farmer Mike Western's shack.

All the other grangers had been against open warfare. Words had got hot between Graham and his neighbors, one openly stating that if Graham caused any trouble between the farmers and the Powers' brand he would hunt down Graham and tend to him himself.

Mel Powers had a spy in the granger ranks. This spy had reported these hot words to his boss. Powers had seen an opening, a way to get the farmers fighting among themselves.

"The farmer said later he'd jump Graham and beat him up if Graham caused any trouble," the spy had said.

So Mel Powers had sent out three gunmen to whip down Si Graham. They'd lure him away by hiding-out his milk-cow. This had apparently happened. And now not only the farmer lay dead in the morgue but also his three gunmen.

What in the hell had happened out there, anyway?

Mel Powers heard foot-sounds come from the hotel door behind him. He glanced at Max, who had turned and looked back. Max's job was to protect the rear; Ted's the front.

"The old witch," Max said.

The old witch was their name for Mickie O'Hannigan, owner of the town's only saloon. Mickie was in her fifties, chunky as a Percheron mare, tough as a green diamond-willow.

Neither man spoke to Mickie. Mickie was a thorn in Mel Powers' side. She was his sworn enemy. She openly admitted that and had openly told Mel Powers that a number of times.

A man's blue shirt covered her heavy front. Well polished riding boots toes protruded from below the cuff of well-creased blue trousers. "Somethin's got you worried, eh, Mel?"

"What'd you mean, Witch?"

"I heard about thet big happy speech you gave them farmers last night. How they were welcome to the Basin an' how they'd raise hay an' you'd buy it an' all would be one big family—a happy family."

"You don't say!"

"But Si Graham got up and said he didn't believe you. Said it wasn't logical you'd willingly give up land you've claimed for years even if Uncle Sam owns it, an' not Half Circle V."

"You don't even sound interesting."

"One farmer there got mad as hell at Graham. Said if Graham didn't keep his mouth shut he might be found dead someday."

"An' then?"

"You figure out the rest," the saloonkeeper said.

The implication was clear. Mickie O'Hannigan implied that Half Circle V had sent out riders to kill Si Graham and lay the blame on the farmer Graham had quarreled with.

"You talk loco!" Mel Powers snarled.

Max stood with a wooden face. Ted watched the woman carefully. Both knew that this woman had long been a thorn in both the sides of the now-dead Powers and his son.

When Warren Powers had driven in his wild Texas longhorns Mickie O'Hannigan was already building her hotel-saloon, the first building in Mad Horse town. Warren powers had soon constructed the rest of the town's buildings and made the town headquarters for his Half Circle V ranch—one reason Cal Sherman had seen no ranch-buildings on the wide expanse of Mad

Horse Basin.

The cowman had tried to buy Mickie out. He wanted complete control of each and every building in town. Mickie wouldn't sell for love nor money.

Warren Powers then tried threats. Mickie laughed at him. Finally the cowman had given up.

Mad Horse town was halfway between Billings and Great Falls. Stages ran through each day, coming and going. Thus until a few months back, Mickie had rented out most of her upstair's rooms each night.

But no more. Last year rails had been laid between the two pioneer towns. These rail had not run through Mad Horse.

Thus the town was cut off, plainly dying. Only one thing could keep the town alive and progressive, and that was farmers moving in.

"These farmers," Mickie told the world in general. "When they come in, the cattle-business will be dead—completely dead except for a few well-blooded stock grazin' behin' bob-wire fences."

"You got somethin' on your mind besides your ugly gray hair," Mel Powers said, eyes narrowed.

Only foor humans were on that porch to hear what Mickie said, and one was Mickie herself. "You're playin' it foxy, Mel Powers. You're waitin' for more farmers to come in an' build dams an' irrigate an' raise alfalfa. Then when the time is right you an' Half Circle V ride in, chase them out—an' you have their fields, all for free."

The twins exchanged glances. Mel Powers said, "God almighty, what a fiendish imagination, woman. You should be writing cowboy stories about how the boys east of the Hudson River think the West is—all blood and gore an' killin's."

Mickie said, "Your sarcasm's wasted, Mel."

Mel Powers said to the twins, "We don't have to listen to this crap." He stepped his white-clothed length down onto the plank sidewalk with Max and Ted walking in the correct positions, one one each side, a pace behind their boss.

Behind them, Mickie laughed sarcastically.

Mel Powers's jaw was stern.

Max said, "She should be silenced."

"That wouldn't be hard to do,' Ted said.

Mel Powers said, "One of you bastards touch a hair on her head and you're as good as dead!"

"You?" Ted asked.

Powers shook his head. "The whole damn' town. They'd jump you an' lynch you before you could say Jack Robinson!"

Max said, "I believe you're right, boss."

"I know I'm right," Mel Powers said shortly.

The trio stopped in front of the hardware store which was no more, the front boarded up. Here was a long bench in the awning's shade. They found seats there, Powers in the middle, the two black-robed gunmen flanking him, a short distance between their rumps and his, as he had ordered.

The old girl was right, Powers thought.

He didn't want to tangle with the farmers. *That'll come later,* he again reasoned; *after there's a bunch in, more reservoirs have been built, more land is under irrigation, and in feed crops. . . .*

He wanted more farmers in, many more. He wanted the entire southern hills made into dams and lakes with farms below, green from irrigation. Say at least a hundred more grangers—more, if possible.

That's why he'd sent out those three to whip the pants

off Si Graham, for above all he wanted peace for at least until the farmers had come and built up this range. . . .

He'd ordered his men to wear masks. And to sneak up on the farmer from behind so's the farmer'd not see their broncs bore Half Circle V irons.

The must have violated my orders. . . .

Four men were cold and dead where none should be. And now the farmers had to be hot under the collars and lusting for combat?

What the hell had gone wrong?

Corpses scattered all over hell's acre out in those god-forsaken hills. Most killed by a rifle—small bore—shooting hard-case bullets, too.

Had a third party moved in with a rifle? Hell, that wasn't logical—or was it, now?

Or was it?

Chapter Four

The town halfwit and other young bucks were kicking broncs out of the chute in one of Half Circle V's corrals when three days later Cal Sherman rode into Mad Horse town.

He came in from the north. He drew in Smoky close to the corral and watched a young punk come out on a blue roan gelding, riding the bronc with only the mane-and-tail hold.

He grinned, and watched.

When a boy down in Arizona Territory, he and his friends had kicked out many a bronc just for the hell of it, riding with the same hold this young gent used.

Riding mane-and-tail you rode bareback. One hand went back for a handful of the bronc's tail-hairs and the other hung onto a hunk of the bronc's mane. Naturally, sooner or later, you got bucked off.

For your grip either loosened on one end or the other. Or you pulled out the hair when the bronc pitched his hardest. And the first thing you knew you were flying through the air, no bucking horse under you.

This happened to this rider at this moment.

He went sailing out, legs spread wide, to land on his rump in the corral dust, the bronc bucking free and kicking at his flanking-strap.

He landed just inside the corral fence. He grinned up at Cal Sherman—a foolish, stupid grin.

There's something missing in his gink, Cal thought and added, mentally, *upstairs*. . . .

For the young man was dressed completely in green. His green old Stetson lay ten feet away in the dust. Sweat pasted his green shirt to his back, his trousers were green as were his old Justin boots.

He didn't get up. He just sat there, legs spread, spurs digging down into the corral dust. "What's your name, stranger?"

Cal noticed a green leather gunbelt circled the thick middle, loops filled with cartridges. The green holster was empty.

Cal gave his name. "And who are you, sir?"

"Sheriff Hank Hawkins."

Cal scowled. "I see you wear no law-star."

"I got one. Over there. Shorty's holdin' it. Didn't want to land on it when this bronc threw me. Pin might go through my heart."

"That's good thinking, Sheriff."

"There's an ol' bastard in town what thinks he's the sheriff. Been walkin' aroun' for years with a star, the phony. What's his name again, Shorty?"

Shorty and the three other young bronc kickers had come to the corral bars to look up at Cal, for evidently a stranger was a rarity in this desolate prairie burg.

"Ike Monday," Shorty said.

"Hell, I thought it was Ike Tuesday," the bronc rider said.

He still sat, staring up at Cal.

Shorty said to Cal, "He's really called the town halfwit, mister, but he insists on thinkin' he's the sheriff."

"He's done thet ever since they kicked him off the stagecoach years ago," another boy said.

Cal's brows rose. "Kicked him from a stage?"

Another boy said, "Yeah, from a stage. He was about four, five, I reckon. Stagedriver got stuck with him. I reckon his mama jus' left him on the stage with her pilin' out somewhere jus' to get rid of him."

"Nobody knows his real name," another said.

One said, "Mickie O'Hannigan took him to feed an' raise. She tried him in the local school but he couldn't learn nothin!"

"He cain't even read and write," Shorty said.

"Who's Mickie O'Hannigan?" Cal asked.

They gave him a complete and up-to-date history on the saloon-keeper. Sheriff Hank Hawkins got to his green boots, dust the dust from his green old trousers, picked up his green hat and was handed his pistol, which also had a green grip.

Cal couldn't make out for sure, but it looked like the .45 was loaded, all six chambers.

That bastard's dangerous, he thought. *A gun doesn't care who handles it, or where it points, or who the hell it kills. . . .*

And a loony doesn't know what he does, either.

"You hear about all them dead men?" Sheriff Hank Hawkins asked, squinting up at Cal, hand on his holstered weapon as Shorty pinned a big tarnished lawman-star on the green shirt.

"I sure haven't," Cal assured.

Sheriff Hawkins explained. Cal listened. "Nobody knows who killed who, or things like that," Sheriff Hank Hawkins said, "But I'm workin' on the case. I'll naturally solve it in time."

"I'm sure you will," Cal assured.

The sheriff squinted up at him. "I cain't recollect seein' you in this town before," he said, "an' I've toted this law-star for forty-four years come next August the fifteenth."

"Just rode in," Cal said.

"Gonna stay a while, drifter?"

"Might and might not. There must be lots of trouble here to have four men killed like you told me, Sheriff."

"Farmers fightin' a cowman. Cowman is Mel Powers. He don't cotton to me or me to him."

"That's not good," Cal said. "All people should get along with the sheriff. Now where could I stable my bronc?"

"He don't 'pear jaded to me."

"Sometimes appearances are deceiving, Sheriff."

"Come in from the north road, eh?"

"That I did. Looking for a punching job."

Sheriff Hawkins shook his head. "Ain't none here. Mel Powers is hirin' guns, not saddle-hands—an' thet gun on your hip ain't hung just right to make a quick draw."

"I'm no hired gun."

"Stick aroun' a little while an' I'll show you how to hang your holster jus' right for a fast draw."

"Nobody can outdraw Mel Powers," Shorty said. "He done shot the bottom part off Max's ear a few months ago."

"Max? His ear?" Cal asked.

He was soon brought to date on that shoot-out, too. "Why everything in green, Sheriff?"

" 'Cause Mel Powers wears only white—always white. An' them two guns of his'n—Max and Ted—they all wear black, always black."

"That's kind of an odd combination," Cal said.

"So I decided on green. All I wear is green, even to my underwear. You want me to pull up my shirt an' show you my green underthings?"

"I'll take your word, Sheriff, Good day, sir, and thank you all for the pleasant conversation."

"Jus' watch your step while you're in my town," Sheriff Hank Hawkins advised.

Cal touched his hat's brim. "That I shall gladly do, Sheriff Hawkins." He rode on, hitting the north end of Mad Horse's two blocks of main street, the only street in town.

While Smoky singlefooted down-street, his rider gave his attention to Mad Horse town.

He was not surprised to see so many buggies, lumber-wagons and spring-wagons in town. From his high spot on the butte he'd seen the farmers head for town, their rigs looking like small ants going downhill toward Mad Horse River and Mad Horse town.

Evidently something stirring in town, he'd thought, remembering the four dead men—and that his .32-20 rifle had killed three of them.

A heavy-set woman wearing pants and a man's shirt and boots stepped down from the hotel porch. This would be Mickie O'Hannigan, he felt sure, and was glad he'd run into Sheriff Hank Hawkins and the young bronc riders.

He drew rein.

The woman now stood on the plank sidewalk. She

looked at him with shrewd eyes.

"Stranger." It was no question. Rather, an affirmation.

Cal Sherman merely nodded.

"Gunman lookin' for Mel Powers? For Half Circle V?" This time it was questions.

Cal Sherman shook his head.

"No other ranch in this basin," the square-built woman said. "You either punch—or sling a gun—for Mel Powers or ride on."

"My bronc is tired. I'm a little saddle-weary myself, Miss O'Hannigan."

The eyes narrowed even more. "How come you know my name, stranger?"

He told of meeting Sheriff Hawkins.

"Oh, Lord," Mickie O'Hannigan said. "What a chore that boy turned out to be. If I'd only known when I took him in all those years back—" She looked down street. "He tell you about the four dead men, all shot to death?"

"He did. And he said he'd solve the mystery of who killed who, or something like that."

"He would."

Cal looked at the farmers' rigs. There were also quite a few saddled horses also eating hitching-post hay. "Town meeting, maybe?"

"Mel Powers called in the farmers. They're meetin' down-street in the school house. I'm headin' there now."

"May I go with you?"

"*May* instead of *can?* My God, man, are you educated, too? I haven't heard *may* used in asking permission since I was kicked out of the sixth grade for swearin' in class, about a hundred years ago. Anyway, it seems like a hundred, at least."

"Sometimes I act almost human," Cal Sherman said. *I better watch my English, or I'll be giving my real job—and work—away. I'd best begin dropping my g's.*

Then he thought, *To hell with that crap . . . I'll speak as I want, and let the damned g's fall where they may!*

"Tie your buckskin to that end of the rack," Mickie O'Hannigan said. "He'll be in the shade there."

The meeting had just been called to order when Cal and the saloon-keeper entered. All seats were occupied so they stood at the back of the room and Mickie introduced him to sheriff Ike Monday.

"He met your counterpart out in Half Circle V's big corral kickin' out cayuses on the mane-and-tail hold," Mickie told the lawman.

Sheriff Monday slowly shook his grizzled head. "Sometimes I think I ought to do somethin' with that boy."

"Like what, say?" Mickie O'Hannigan's voice had acquired a sharp tone. "Send him over to Warm Springs, mebbe?"

Before heading north, Cal Sherman had read all he could find on Montana. Therefore he knew that the state mental hospital was many miles west in the Rocky Mountains at Warm Springs.

"That wouldn't be a bad idea," the lawman said.

"You ship him there an' you ship me with 'im!"

"That ain't a bad idea, either," the sheriff assured.

Cal turned his attention to the speaker. He judged him one of the gun-twins for he was dressed in solid black. "What twin is that?" he asked.

"Cain't see his ears so I cain't tell," Mickie replied.

A bench was behind the lectern next to the wall. A tall young man in dazzling white sat at its south end. Beside him was another twin, black and dangerous. On the far end opposite the twin sat a man plainly a farmer.

This chunky forty-year-old wore a faded blue shirt, tub-washed dim-colored overalls. Heavy lace boots encased his big feet.

"Who's the farmer?" Cal asked Mickie.

"That's Mike Western. The farmers held the meetin' at his shack when Mel Powers told them he wanted more in the basin. When Si Graham made fun of Powers he got in trouble with Western."

"Hot words, eh?"

"Hot, an' then some. Western claimed he'd kill Graham if Graham made trouble between the grangers an' Half Circle V."

"Maybe Western killed Graham?"

"Impossible. He spent the night in my hotel. Gambled until midnight, then got a room upstairs."

Cal Sherman nodded. "That should clear him. But what about all these three dead Half Circle V men lying around a dead Si Graham?"

"That's the mystery," the saloon keeper said. "Got everybody stumped, especially this sheriff here."

"You mention me?" Sheriff Monday said sharply.

"Only in an appraisin' way, of course, sheriff," the woman said.

"You two are talkin' too much," the sheriff said. "I can't hear all bein' said."

"You ain't missin' nothing," Mickie O'Hannigan said.

"I'm goin' down front to hear," the sheriff said.

Mickie O'Hannigan watched the broad back move away. "As humans go, Ike Monday's a good man—but as a sheriff, he never was much. Ol' Warren Powers got him his job an' kept him in office all these years. This town needs a whole new bunch in the court house, includin' a new sheriff."

Cal gave his attention to the speaker. The twin was a good talker. He spoke in clear, loud tones.

Cal then noticed he read from a paper on the lectern. He supposed Mel Powers—or mebbeso Half Circle V's lawyer—had written the speech.

The Powers' ranch again emphasized it welcomed farmers. Half Circle V and the farmers would work together.

The farmers would raise fodder for Half Circle V's cattle. Last winter too many Powers' cattle had died from winter-kill. Had they had hay and protection from blizzards they'd have pulled through.

Half Circle V was going to sell off its steers and bulls this fall. The Powers ranch was shipping in full-blooded Hereford and Shorthorn bulls to breed up the beef crop.

Cal Sherman looked over the audience. He saw a glistening red head. He remembered seeing it bent over a dead man. "Who's the red head?"

"Bea Graham. Si Graham's daughter. Si had two children. The boy sittin' next to the daughter is named Bill, I believe. About sixteen or aroun' there, I'd judge."

"How'd he take his father's death?"

"Claims he'll kill whoever killed his father. Only thing is—who the hell killed him? An' who the hell killed those three Powers' stiffs. This ain't logical—three other dead men."

"Nobody has any idea?"

"They first figured Western had ridden out an' done the shootin', but he was in my hotel all night. I know that."

"How come you know for sure?"

"I sleep with my door open at the head of the stairs. Too many of the sonsofbitches have tiptoed past, with boots in hand, an' escaped without payin' their bills. Western was in thet room all night."

"This don't make sense. Mebbeso they all got fightin' an' shot each other to death?"

"That don't make sense, either. Don't seem logical all would get killed, an' what would they be fightin' about?"

"I dunno. None of my never-mind."

"Mrs. Graham is home in bed. Shocked, I'd say. Hey, drifter, you lookin' for a job?"

"I need to eat. And to eat, you got have a little jingle."

"My day bartender jerked stakes a coupla days back. I bin tendin' bar myself an' thet's a job I don't cotton to. Two bucks a day, four shots of booze—but after or before shift, an' room upstairs an' found."

"You hired a bartender."

"You ever tend bar before? You know how to mix drinks?"

"Always been on the paying side, Miss O'Hannigan, but I can learn. I went to the second reader in school."

"Educated man," the woman said. "You start in the mornin'. Later on I'll show you how to mix a few drinks an' your room upstairs."

"I thank you, lady." Cal again looked at the speaker. "That twin is as windy as William Jennings Bryan."

"He ain't makin' thet up. He's readin' it."

The twin finished speaking. He'd summed up a good case for Half Circle V, Cal Sherman guessed.

Farmer Mike Western got up and took over the lectern.

Western had only a few words. He emphasized the

fact he'd played poker the night after the meeting in Mickie's saloon. He'd gone to bed upstairs and had slept until nine the next morning.

"Miss O'Hannigan is at the end of the hall," the farmer said, "an' I feel sure she will back up my statement."

All necks turned. All eyes landed on Mickie and Cal. Mickie said, "Mr. Western slept until nine, as he says, in my hotel."

"How do you know?"

The words came from young Bill Graham.

Mickie told about her open door. "Nobody gets past me without payin' his bill."

"Amen to that," a masculine voice said. "I tried that once—an' never got off home-plate!"

A few tittered at this, but laughter was short and low. Grimness held these people—these Half Circle V cowboys, the farmers, the townspeople. A few days before the gut wagon had carried four dead men to the village cemetery.

The farmer said, "That's all I have to say," and sat down.

Sheriff Ike Monday then took charge. He asked if anybody else had anything to say.

Young Bill Graham started to his feet. By sheer force, his red headed sister bore him down.

"You keep what you think to yourself," she said sternly.

"My father—Your father, too. He's in that grave—An' someday I'll kill whoever put him there—"

"You hush, and right now."

"Okay, sis." Grudgingly.

"Nothin' more?" the sheriff asked.

One of the twins got to his boots. "I have a request,

Sheriff, from Mr. Powers."

The sheriff scowled. "Name it, please."

The twin looked across the heads at Cal Sherman. "There is a stranger standing beside Miss O'Hannigan," he said.

"What about him?" the sheriff asked.

"Mr. Powers is curious. Strangers seldom come into town now that the railroad is built."

"Come to the point, sir?"

"Mr. Powers wants to know the stranger's name. He wants to know how long he's been on this range and what his business is in Mad Horse."

All eyes bore down on Cal Sherman.

Chapter Five

Cal Sherman's lips tightened. "You speaking to me?

"I am."

"Do you talk for yourself? Or do you talk for that man dressed in white beside you?"

"I speak for the man in white. He's my boss."

"Why don't you tell him a thing or two?"

"Like what?"

"Tell him to speak for himself. He's a big boy now—or at least, he looks to be, so he should be able to speak for himself."

Mickie O'Hannigan murmured, "You're lookin' for trouble, fella."

"Let it come."

The black-garbed gunman said, "Maybe Mr. Powers doesn't want to speak to you?"

"Then why the hell did you point me out?"

Necks craned. Eyes watched. Silence held the hall. Cal saw Powers and the gunman converse quietly for a long moment, Mel Powers' eyes on Cal. Finally the white-dressed cowman got to his boots.

He crossed the platform. He stepped down. He came down the aisle toward Cal with Cal watching him carefully.

White boots made heel-sounds on the floor. White clad legs moved forward. Cal heard the creak of the white gunbelt and holsters.

The white-dressed man had a dangerous aura around him. Never for one moment did Cal Sherman underestimate this fast-gun.

Mel Powers stopped in front of Mickie O'Hannigan and Cal.

The saloon-keeper quietly warned, "Watch yourself, Mel Powers!"

Powers did not take his eyes off Cal Sherman. His thin lips parted. "Thanks for the warnin', old witch."

He hissed his words. They dripped sarcasm.

"Why don't you say the word as you think it?" the saloon-keeper asked.

"What word?"

"Witch. Start with a *b* instead of a *w*, like you'd like to."

Mel Powers laughed soundlessly. "You don't count," he said and stopped in front of Cal Sherman. "Your name, stranger?"

"That's my business."

Powers slowly shook his head. "You're wrong there, stranger. Your name is my business."

"What makes you say that?"

"You're in Mad Horse town. You're on Mad Horse range. I own this town and this range is mine."

"You don't figure right," Cal pointed out.

Powers watched him. He was dead-panned and yet under his studied insolence Cal Sherman glimpsed controled power—power that with the right provocation would result in red roaring guns.

"Straighten out my thinkin', stranger?"

"Except for homesteaded land, this land belongs not to you but to Uncle Sam," Cal said.

"You've never heard of squatter's rights?"

The hall was very, very quiet. Farmers stood and watched and Sheriff Ike Monday stood beside Mickie O'Hannigan, who stood close at Cal's right.

"I have. The theory is that the first to squat on the land owns the land, but courts all over the west have declared that a false premise—and the cowman has lost, each and every time."

"You talk big, stranger." Mel Powers balanced himself on his white boots and Sheriff Ike Monday said sharply, "Watch how you handle your hands, Mel! Watch where you put 'em!"

Powers spoke from the corner of his mouth. "Watch your words, Ike. If you don't watch them, you'll be outa a job an' so help me god I'll have Hank Hawkins really an' truly sportin' a star."

That brought a nervous laugh from the front of the hall.

Powers said, "You handle words, stranger. Now mebbeso you can handle your horse jus' as well as you can your tongue?"

This was Cal's turn to laugh shortly. "You ordering me out of town, Powers?"

"I might an' I might not—What the hell is this?"

For a young man had barged between Cal and the cowman. He wore all green and he plunged between him, pistol in hand. He buried his shoulder in Mel Powers' belly.

Powers went backwards, caught his balance, rage

flaring across his face. "You little sonofabitch—"

He swung a right. It missed and again a billy-goat butted the rancher in the belly. Sheriff Ike Monday came in, getting his bulk between Powers and the loony.

Mickie O'Hannigan leaped on Sheriff Hank Hawkins, her weight almost bearing him to the floor. She pinned both arms around his from behind and fairly lifted him from the floor.

"Son, son, watch yourself, please!"

Sheriff Hank Hawkins struggled for freedom, but his foster mother held him securely. She did a good job, Cal saw. He then realized that naturally during her many years as a saloon-keeper she'd thrown many a drunk from her establishment with a similar hold.

The real sheriff spoke to Cal Sherman. "Stranger, do me a favor? Please leave right now. My office is down street, south. It's open. I'll meet you there."

"That's what it is."

"Okay, Sheriff." Cal Sherman got lazily afoot. He started for the door. His right boot shot out, hooked under the swivel-chair, and upended it and the sheriff.

"Excuse me, Sheriff."

Sheriff Ike Monday landed on his back. He reached for his holster but his gun had slid out and he found only air in his grasp.

Sheriff Monday got to his feet. "You—" He paused, staring beyond Cal, who had frozen in his tracks, something hard and round against his back, just below its middle.

"Put your hands up, stranger!"

Cal recognized the voice of Sheriff Hank Hawkins. His hands rose automatically. He looked at Sheriff Ike Monday.

"Put thet damn' gun down, you fool kid, or I'll—"

"You'll what?" Sheriff Hawkins demanded. "I'm roddin' this deal an'—" He never got to finish his sentence.

For Cal Sherman had gone into fast and violent action. Rough Riders were taught early in training never to stick a gun into a man's back. Always keep a short distance away.

The reasoning was simple. When you had a gun against a man, he could whirl and swing to one side and the gun would slip forward—and the man could catch you with a hard fist or the barrel of his gun.

Or even empty his short-gun in your guts. . . .

It happened in a mere few seconds. Cal's rising right fist landed hard on the loony's jaw. It sent him reeling. Before Sheriff Hawkins knew what had happened, Cal Sherman had the loony's short-gun.

Cal broke the breech. Cartridges were kicked out—but none had leads. Cal realized he'd hit the would-be sheriff as hard as he could hit and now he wished he hadn't, but how could he have known the cartridges were dead?

"Okay, Sheriff."

He was slouched in a chair when Sheriff Ike Monday a few minutes later wheeled in his bulk to collapse in his swivel chair. "Hot as the hinges of hell." The lawman mopped his forehead with a dirty blue bandana. "You must wanta get killed, stranger."

"He pushed me," Cal Sherman reminded.

"He's got a habit of doin' that. He knows all the time his gun will back 'im up. You heard about him shootin' thet ear off, ain't you?"

"Your other sheriff told me."

"When?"

Cal related facts.

"Mind if I ask what is your bizness in our town?" the sheriff asked.

"Not a bit. I'm going to tend bar days for Miss O'Hannigan. She hired me just a few minutes ago."

"Yeah, she needs a day man. Ol' Ric Snow left in a hell of a hurry a few days back. Had a few words with one of the twins."

"Powers and his twins have the town treed, eh?"

The sheriff shook his head. "Powers owns every buildin' in town except Mickie's joint, so you can't tree somethin' you own."

"I disagree. A man trees through fear, not ownership of buildings. And if I read this right, this town is afraid—and really afraid."

"Of Mel Powers?"

"Of Mel Powers, yes."

"You're new here," the sheriff said. "Your jus' makin' guesses. You don't know this town an' these people. Mind if I give you a bit of advice, stranger?"

"My ears are open."

"Don't take that bartendin' job. Get your big buckskin an' ride out an' don't come back."

"That an order?"

"You hit the boy awful hard," Monday accused.

"How'd I to know his shells weren't loaded? What if he'd had real cartridges? Was I just to stand there—get shot from behind?"

"Where'd you learn thet trick?" Monday asked.

"From Wild Bill Hickock."

Sheriff Monday studied him. "Come with another. Wild Bill got kilt some twenty five years or so over in the Dakotas. Twenty five years ago you weren't big enough to handle a gun."

Cal didn't answer. He helped a dazed Sheriff Hawkins to his boots. "What happened to me?"

"You stumbled. You knocked yourself cold," Cal seriously informed.

Sheriff Hank Hawkins rubbed his jaw. "I remember now. Horse kicked me in the jaw—back in the corral."

"That's right," Cal said.

"Saw the hoof comin', too—but couldn't duck in time. You carried me in here, stranger?"

"That I did," Cal assured.

"I'd better go see the doc," Sheriff Hawkins said.

Cal didn't know whether the youth was putting on an act or just didn't remember. For some reason he got the impression this boy was not as loony as he put on.

Why did he think this? He didn't know for sure.

He escorted Sheriff Hawkins to the door. Meanwhile he segregated one of the double eagles in his pant's pocket from the five others.

Sheriff Hank Hawkins didn't see Cal slip the double eagle into his shirt pocket. Neither did the real sheriff—Sheriff Ike Monday—see the fast act. Sheriff Hawkins left.

Cal looked at Sheriff Monday. Monday was rubbing his wide butt. "You still ordering me out of town?" Cal asked.

"I could jug you."

"On what charge?"

"Vagrancy, for one."

Cal laughed. "You forget I got a job. And a man with a job can't very well be pinched for being a vagrant. You'll have to think of a better charge than that, sheriff."

"You got a reason for bein' in this town."

"I have, huh? Well, how nice. What ever gave you that wild idea, might I ask?"

"You talk like an educated man. There's more than mere chance behin' your bein' here."

"Don't work your imagination overtime. I wish you well." Cal stepped out into the boiling late morning sun.

He stood for a long moment under the wooden awning, his eyes moving across Mad Horse town—and despite the boarded up buildings and the dust and dogs sleeping in the shade, he liked what he saw.

This area had great promise. Miles and miles of fertile land surrounded this cowtown. That land was good Montana sagebrush-growing land and not greasewood growing.

From what he'd read in Uncle Sam's journals from the Agriculture Department crops grew good on sagebrush land . . . if they had the water. But not so on land growing the scraggly greasewood plant.

But sagebrush grew only on good sandy soil. And he'd taken careful note and he'd not seen a greasewood on this basin.

All this land needed to make this a well-to-do and productive town was tillage and water.

For this area lacked enough rainfall to be changed into productive farming country. What few inches of rain it had in a year came usually in the winter in the form of snow.

The few drops of rain that fell in the summer were not enough to grow crops, either head-crops or soil-crops such as spuds. To farm here—and farm profitably and properly—you'd have to have irrigation.

Uncle Sam wanted this land settled. Uncle Sam would send out engineers to survey canyons and coulees for possible storage dams, like those he'd seen along the southern foothills.

He remembered one of the twins telling the farmers they were welcome. Cal Sherman had doubted this when he'd heard it. The man in the white suit with the white-handled sixguns was not going to give away his range without a struggle.

Then what did Mel Powers have in mind?

Get the land settled, the water stored, and then run the farmers off? Cal Sherman couldn't believe this. This basin get full of fences and windmills and farmers and tilled soil—

Powers could never run that many people off. And, besides, he didn't own this land and—

Cal Sherman scowled. Something was wrong here. Something was amiss. His mind searched over all he'd read. Squatter's rights was a dead monkey. Mel Powers didn't appear to be a fool. He'd sure know that, wouldn't he?

Anyhow, he liked Mad Horse Basin. And he'd make a stand here and work and try to grow up with the country—if indeed it became a land of nice homes and good families.

Later on he'd discuss these things with Mickie for she was an old-timer here and she knew this range and its people.

He'd noticed that a lot of the men in the school house had worn cowpuncher gear—chaps, spurs, boots, big hats and guns. He had judged them to be Powers' hands. Most looked like they were no strangers to the grip of a side-arm.

He walked south. Whenever he came to a building with boards over the windows he peered between the cracks.

He was looking into one deserted building when he heard a buggy stop in the street behind him. He turned quickly, hand going to his holster—and then stopping.

For the buggy seat held but one man. He was the

farmer, Mike Western. "I'd like to talk to you a minute, if I can, Mr.—"

"Sherman, Mr. Western. Cal Sherman."

"I'm Mike Western."

Cal nodded. "Recognized you from the meeting. Something I can do for you, sir?"

"Thought mebbeso you'd like details of the meetin' held at my house, the night before all them dead men was found."

"That's hardly any business of mine."

"Heard you was goin' tend bar for Mickie. Thought you might hear a lot of talk an' I want to put the record straight."

Cal nodded.

"Si Graham got hot at thet meetin'. Mel Powers took it like a man. He never got mad at Graham, even though Graham did throw some wicked words his direction about Half Circle V."

Cal nodded.

"Aim to stay on this range long, Mr. Sherman?"

Cal gave this situation brief study. Western had no reason to stop and gossip with him. He didn't like the farmer's looks. Western was small, thin, rat-faced and had shifty gray eyes.

Cal studied the farmer. "You ask a lot of questions. Now I'll ask one. How long do you expect to stay in Mad Horse Basin?"

Western went red-faced. "Sorry I bothered you!" He clucked to his team. He drove away without another word.

Cal Sherman watched the farmer leave. He had the thing figured out, now. Mel Powers was telling the farmers a big lie. He didn't want them in Mad Horse basin.

He just acted as though he wanted them. They'd gone far enough. They'd made dams and run out irrigation ditches and had good alfalfa fields. They'd done their work.

Now it was time to get shut of them?

Graham and Western had quarreled. They had threatened each other. Powers had moved in that morning. He'd sent out gunmen to kill Graham and lay the blame on Western.

Nobody could prove that Western had not left his hotel room by a window, dropped to the ground, ridden out to kill Graham—then had returned to his room, tiptoeing past the sleeping Mickie O'Hannigan.

But Powers hadn't figured that another gun—the gun of one Cal Sherman—would move into the play, totally by accident.

Townspeople had found a dead Si Graham. They'd also found three dead Powers' gunmen.

They could think but one thing: Powers had sent out guns to kill Si Graham. If he hadn't, why had the dead gunmen been scattered around like they'd been—those Half Circle V gunhands?

Cal put himself in the boots of one of the townspeople. That person would come to only one conclusion. During the gunfight Si Graham had managed to kill each and every one of Powers' gundogs.

Then, and only then, had the wounded Si Graham dropped dead.

Cal Sherman's blood froze. If Powers ever discovered that he, Cal Sherman, had killed Snodgrass, Hersey and Martin—

Cal's life wouldn't be worth a plugged nickel. The guns of the twins and the guns of Mel Powers would send him hurling into Kingdom Come.

He remembered the gold pieces. He'd been a damned fool to pick those off the dead gunmen. By so doing he'd the same as told Mel Powers that another party besides Si Graham had become involved in the blood-soaked mess.

And, unless he was completely cockeyed, Mel Powers would be keeping an ear to the ground and both eyes wide open to try to discover who that third party had been.

And naturally, suspicion had fallen on him, because he was a stranger. He gave that some thought, then realized Mel Powers would be suspicious of others, maybe even some townspeople?

He continued downstreet peering into deserted buildings. He was carefully studying a room holding an old upright printing-press when once again he heard hoofs behind him.

This time it was a young man on an old gray horse that Cal immediately recognized, even to old army saddle and bridle with blinders. He remembered the old horse thundering through the brush, the reins whipping out to wrap around a bootheel and send him on his behind.

"Cal Sherman here," Cal said. "And you?"

"Bill Graham. My father was the farmer killed three days ago."

Cal studied the boy. He judged him to be sixteen—lanky, flat-bellied, with a studious thin face.

"None of my business, Bill,' Cal said.

"I know that, Mr. Sherman. But you're new here and Mr. Powers challenged you, back in the school."

"That he did," Cal said.

"He's a dangerous man. And he had no reason to talk to you as he did. To me it looks like he's out to get you, Mr. Sherman."

"Why do you say that?"

The trio marched in strict military order. Cal Sherman almost winced, remembering the Rough Riders who had stormed San Juan Hill sans horses and with their leader safely a mile out at sea watching through a telescope while newspapers printed pictures of him leading his men up-slope against the Spanish's Mauser rifles.

"They always walk that way?" he asked Bill Graham.

"Ever since I can remember, but I ain't been here long—an' won't be much longer."

Cal had a sudden thought. "Before your mother sells to Western I'd like to have a chance at your homestead."

"You aim to farm?"

"I might. Cowpunching days are over."

"That ain't what Mel Powers thinks. I'll tell Ma about you. Gotta get on my way, now."

"Your missing cow?"

"She was five miles from home. Somebody must've chased her to lure Pa into thet brush."

"I see."

The boy turned the old horse and rode away high on the stirrups of the old cavalry saddle. Cal knew why the boy stood on high stirrups. The buckles and steel on the saddle's bed raised calluses on a man's behind where calluses had no right to be.

He knew . . . from experience.

Cal looked up-street at Powers and the twins. They wheeled and entered a building. Cal had in passing noticed a sign on the window proclaiming its insides housed the headquarters of Half Circle V ranch.

"Two points, sir. Powers watches every man who comes into this region, especially more so a stranger. Second, he jumped you at the meetin' for no valid reason, or so it seemed to me."

Cal nodded, listening. He'd gathered the same impression. He had wondered then, as he now did, if other eyes had seen him three mornings ago when he'd killed in self-defense three of Mel Powers' gun-riders.

"Perhaps you imagine things, Bill."

"Why say that?"

"Well, your father's death, for one thing—You've had a rough experience. A man's imagination—at such times—"

"I understan', Mr. Sherman. We're leavin' the country—Ma, my sister, an' me."

"Your farm?"

"Mr. Western has offered us a price. Not a good price, but a fair one. We'll leave inside of a week, at least."

Cal studied the studious face. He put it into his memory, line by line, feature by feature—and at that time, wondered why he went to such lengths. He said, "I wish you and yours well, Mr. Graham."

"Look up street, sir."

Cal looked. Mel Powers and the twins had just left Mickie O'Hannigan's saloon. They walked toward him, two blocks away.

Mel Powers' white-clad toughness walked deliberately in the middle of the plank walk making whoever he met step to one side or even off the planks into the street's thick dust.

His black-garbed gun-guard kept a pace behind and a few paces out. They strode with deadly solemness. They personified guns and gunsmoke and lead and death. Yes, death—always death. . . .

He heard boots approaching. He looked about and then realized they came from the space between this building and the next.

Sheriff Hank Hawkins emerged. "Did I scare the bejeepers outa you, Cal?" He grinned satanically.

"Plumb outa my boots, Sheriff Hawkins."

"I got a handful of lawmen helpin' me clean up sin in this town, you know. We'll all have green uniforms in a couple of days. Ma measured us all a couple of weeks ago an' ordered them from Saws an' Roebun."

"That's good."

"I got a undersheriff—Shorty—an' six deputies. You got any idea what a undersheriff is, an' what makes him different than a deputy?"

Cal scratched his head, apparently thinking. *This young bastard isn't as loco as they say he is.*

"Let me see, now . . . Oh, yes, the undersheriff is next to the sheriff in importance, the deputies below him. Mind me now, I once had to kill me a undersheriff. Kept bothering me. Shot him dead, one shot, right through the brisket—and his bullet missed by a miles."

"I don't cotton to thet, but we'll let it pass. All of us got some liar in us, I reckon. But thet ain't what I come to talk to you about."

"You going to put me under arrest?"

"Not right now, but you're on dangerous ground. An' if I throw you in the cooler it'll be to pertect you."

"What do you mean by that, Sheriff Hawkins?"

"Well, you an' Mr. Powers had thet ruckus in the school-house. I figure you'd a-gone for guns if'n I hadn't horned in."

"I thank you for your help, Sheriff."

"I want to warn you to be on guard. Powers was insulted there an' he's got them damn' twins—Well, you understan', don't you?"

"I sure do."

Sheriff Hawkins turned to leave, then stopped. "A queer thing happened a few minutes back when I was in Aunt Mickie's saloon."

"And that?"

"Put my han' in my shirt pocket. Aimed to twist me a quirley. I carry my Durham in my shirt pocket."

Cal nodded.

"Well, out come the Durham. An' you know what else popped out with it?"

"Ain't got no idea."

"A gold double eagle. Twenty bucks. Most money I ever had in my life. Mel Powers said the same."

"Powers saw the money?"

"He sure did. Asked to look at it. I let him but I watched him damn' close to see he didn't pocket it."

"What'd he say?"

"He studied the gold. Then handed it back. He never said a word. I bought drinks for the house."

Cal nodded.

"I know how that money got there," Sheriff Hawkins said.

"How?"

The youth grinned crookedly. "Came from heaven, Mr. Suckerland. God dropped it in my pocket." He turned to go, then pivoted and said, "Sometimes hit me again in the jaw, eh?"

"Why?"

Sheriff Hank Hawkins laughed and stalked away, green garbed and with a green-handled six-shooter. Cal went between the two buildings so nobody would see him as he took one of the gold coins from his pocket and studied it very carefully.

He carefully studied the coin. At first he noticed nothing out of the ordinary. And then he saw something that made his blood jump.

For the coin's rim sported three tiny notches, apparently made by a small three-cornered file. Somebody had deliberately marked the gold.

He looked hurriedly about. Nobody watched. He dug out the remaining eagles. Each was so marked. He put them back in his pocket, forehead grooved.

Quickly he added points.

Somebody had marked these gold pieces. And why? That answer came readily. They were marked so they could be identified.

And why would anybody want to identify the gold later on? He found no answer to that question. The gold had come from the bodies of three dead gunmen.

Those gunmen had slung guns for Mel Powers. It then stood to reason Powers had marked the coins?

Then, it hit him.

Sheriff Harry Hawkins' life was in danger. And he, Cal Sherman, had put the green-clad would-be lawman under the gun. Mel Powers' gun. . . .

When that gold piece had tumbled from Sheriff Hawkins' pocket Mel Powers would have figured the would-be sheriff had robbed the bodies of his gunmen. He could think nothing different.

He'd blame Sheriff Hawkins for the killings. Cal cursed his luck. He'd meant to help the young fellow. Instead of that he'd led him into a deadly gun-trap.

Then another terrible thought hit him.

Had Sheriff Hawkins seen him slip the gold-piece into his pocket? If so, the would-be sheriff would know that he, Cal Sherman, had taken the gold from the dead gunmen.

Cal soon abandoned this fear. Had Sheriff Harry Hawkins seen him drop the double-eagle in Hawkin's short-pocket Hawkins would have immediately blurted out something.

And he's said nothing. He'd not noticed. Then, had the real sheriff—obese Ike Monday—seen him drop the coin into the pocket?

He felt safe, there. His body had been between the real sheriff and the pseudo sheriff. Monday'd not seen.

And what had been Mel Powers' reaction on seeing the gold? His mind went back to Sheriff Hawkins' words. Powers had said nothing. Just handed back the gold, nothing more.

Powers evidently had been surprised. Anybody would have appeared surprised at learning that his young loco with an empty gun had apparently killed what must of been three fast gunmen.

Powers was evidently thinking this over.

The gold pieces had suddenly become dangerous. This was a bushwhack range. What if somebody came in behind him, pistol raised?

And that pistol came down on his skull, knocking him cold? And the man who'd slugged him then searched his pockets?

And found this tell-tale gold?

Cal realized he'd have to get shut of these eagles, and damn' soon. Bury them somewhere?

Throw them into Mad Horse River?

His conservative nature rebelled against forever destroying the gold. Money was scarce in this economic depression. Many people here in town would welcome with glee even one gold piece.

He'd drop them unnoticed around town. The damage had already been done. It could not be recalled.

What had started out as a good-will gesture had turned into a death-signal. For Sheriff Harry Hawkins was in only one position.

That of death . . .

Chapter Six

Fat Sheriff Monday sat gingerly in his swivel chair when dusk crept in that night. He favored his huge left buttock.

That's the one he'd landed on when that damn' stranger had pulled the chair out from under him.

The day had been unbearably hot. Now with sundown it was just as hot, if not hotter. There was no breeze. The only time the wind stopped blowing in Montana, he again thought, was for a few brief moments at sunrise and again at sundown.

You couldn't light a lamp. If you did millions of mosquitoes—yes, millions—would storm his old office. And, even with a screen door and screen windows, a few hundred somehow would manage to enter.

And these Montana mosquitoes had bills like a woodpecker. Once they hit you, they opened not veins but arteries. Out on the range the range-horses were running hell-for-leather for some shady spot—like in a grove of thick trees—where there'd been deposited a lot of manure.

Mosquitoes won't enter a dark spot where there is the smell of manure, the sheriff knew.

Sheriff Ike Monday belched. His belly was acting up again. It always got on its high-horse when trouble arose. And what had been a peaceful range just a few months back was now nothing but trouble.

Holy god, four dead men in one morning, think of that! And who in the name of billy-hell had killed whom and for why?

And now this other stupidity. . . .

For instance, that damned loony—Coming up all of a sudden with a new shiny twenty buck gold pice. Now where in all get-out had that loco ever got that gold piece?

He'd not been in the saloon when the double-eagle had fallen but a town male gossip had reported back.

"Mel picks up thet gold piece. He looks at it like he'd never seen gold afore—an' him a rich young man, too!"

"He ask the loony where he'd got it?"

The gossip had tugged his gray beard. "Min' now, I'm not sure. My own eyes was at the point of fallin' out. If I recollect correct, Mel didn't ask but jes' handed the gold back."

Sheriff Ike Monday shifted slightly to ease the strain on his injured buttock.

And all these other gold pieces that suddenly had come to life. . . .

All found by townspeople . . . And all double eagles, too. . . . He'd doubted the stories at first. And then he'd personally seen three of the gold pieces. And seeing was believing, wasn't it?

Worthless old man Sessions, the town bum. . . . Session had just an hour ago found a double-eagle laying next to the gate leading up to his miserable tarpaper and tin *jacal*.

He'd seen that gold piece. Sessions was down at the saloon now drinking it up and setting up drinks. Mickie O'Hannigan would soon have that gold but hell, didn't Mickie get almost all the town's extra money, in the end?

Sheriff Ike Monday had been in Mickie's when old man Sessions had busted in with the gold clutched in his wizened hand. Mel Powers had been there, too. And right off Mel had grabbed the gold and looked long and hard at it—and why had he done that?

Then Missus Granville Smith's new baby. . . . Settin' there in his home-made little corral suckin' a gold piece—a double-eagle—when his mama had come out. She'd rushed over in a hell of a hurry. Pulled the gold piece outa the kid's grip jus' as he was gonna put it down is gullet. Prob'ly saved the little bastard's life, his mama did. . . .

Mel had been in his office when news of this event arrived. He'd immediately sent one of the twins—the one with the good ears—over to give twenty bucks in silver dollars for the gold piece.

What was Mel doing? Collecting gold?

And all of a sudden old man Jackson and that old sot, Mrs. Beeman, had suddenly appeared at Mickie's joint, both asking a private conference back in Mickie's office.

When their meetings were over both then repaired to Mickie's bar with plenty of silver and began a week long drunk.

Somebody claimed they'd traded twenty dollar gold pieces for silver with Mickie, trying to keep secret the fact they'd had some money—for each owed about everybody in town a few cents and they didn't want their creditors swarming down on them—alcohol came before payment of just debts.

If this was true, that made five who'd suddenly acquired gold. Where had the gold pieces come from?

Sheriff Ike Monday shrugged.

His thoughts went to tall Cal Sherman. Sherman evidently wasn't a man whom you could push around. He'd shown that fact in this office a few hours back.

Why had Sherman come to Mad Horse town?

Was he a rep from Uncle Sam? Sent out by Uncle to see how the homesteaders were faring? He'd heard of such down in Wyoming when the cowmen had smoked out—and killed—Nate Champion and a friend some years before.

Uncle Sam now watched to see none of his homesteaders was killed by cowman. Uncle Sam wanted people to move west. Uncle Sam's cities back east were getting so over-populated that gangs there spent their time murdering peaceful citizens or other gangs, he'd read.

Had this Sherman gink ridden in to see that Mel Powers didn't mistreat the farmers?

He'd made an error in talking rough to this Sherman bucko. He sighed and climbed laboriously to his boots. Time to refuel the old motor. The Steerhorn Cafe and Effie Lincoln's endless chatter or Mickie O'Hannigan's dining room, the only two eating places in town?

He decided on Mickie's. Effie had been after him and had openly asked him to marry her, even when his wife had been alive. And who wanted an empty-headed old magpie around his house?

He waddled down-street, hating every plank in the

sidewalk, every board in every building, every shingle on every roof. Across the street he saw Sheriff Hank Hawkins and his undersheriff and three of his deputies. He gave them a scornful look and lumbered on.

Time I quit the sonsofbitches, he told himself. *I've managed to save some money, moreso since the Old Lady did me the good turn of dying on me. . . .*

And a man in public office always managed somehow to cut himself a little bit in on the county's money without anybody proving it. They might suspect but to suspect and prove are two different points, sometimes miles and miles apart.

He had his graft hidden in an Omaha, Nebraska, bank. His wife had an old school chum there, a heavy-set woman who'd lost her husband about the time his old magpie had kicked the bucket.

One letter had led to another. Of course a guy never had to marry it. He could stop for a few days, sample her wares and then, if the scene was a bit unhealthy or unhappy, a man could catch the rails and ride on.

He glanced at Sheriff Hank Hawkins. The sheriff had his undersheriff sitting on the Merc's steps. He apparently was lecturing his men on some of the finer points of criminal detection.

Sheriff Ike Monday grinned ruefully. He'd be the last to admit it but Sheriff Hank Hawkins definitely knew more about criminals and criminal habits than he did.

Sheriff Hawkins subscribed to a number of law-enforcement magazines. He and his staff read them from kiver-to-kiver. If he and the other sheriff were to write an examination—or paper—on law enforcement, he was sure Sheriff Hawkins would win.

He came to the office of Half Circle V ranch and he looked in. The twins were sitting and staring out the door. He got on the left side of one and saw he had a good ear-lobe and he said, "Where's the boss, Ted?"

"Damn' if I know."

Max said, "Out huntin' gold."

Sheriff Monday forced a hollow laugh. He'd never felt at home around these two dangerous guns. "What's this crap about all them gol' pieces turnin' up?"

Max told him what he already knew.

"Judgin' from thet," Sheriff Monday said, "Five people foun' gold pieces layin' aroun' if it's true thet ol' Jed Jackson an' Mrs. Harry Beeman traded gold to Mickie for common money."

"That they did," Ted said.

Max felt of his left ear. "Mike Western seen them go into Mickie's office. She left the door open. Western saw Mickie give them silver money."

Sheriff Monday knew that was mere gossip. In the first place, Mickie always kept her office door shut. *An' besides, she'd be sure to shut it if something that important took place.*

"Thought Western left town," the sheriff said.

Western's off-horse had acquired a limp. He'd turned his rig around and driven back into town and was at the bar now, Ted informed.

"You don't know where Mel is, then?" the sheriff asked.

"I tol' you the truth, starman," Max growled. "He's out huntin' gold. To see if more of them twenty-buck gold pieces has fell from heaven. He's awful interested in money, you know."

The sheriff said, "Name a person who isn't," and he walked on, thinking of the farmer Mike Western.

He hadn't attended the meeting four nights back the farmers had held in Western's shack. He'd not been notified of the meeting. He reasoned that his office should have been so informed. He judged it a slight to the county sheriff's office.

He'd heard from one farmer—Carl Hanson—that although things seemed normal, there had been an underfeeling of anger among the farmers. Their nerves were getting raw, the Swede had mentioned.

"It's this Mel Powers, Sher'ff. Always in the background, grinnin' like a sick ape—but a dangerous ape. It ain't logical he'd want farmers on his range."

"I think it is," the sheriff had said.

"Explain, please?"

"He needs hay for winter feed. He's changin' his ranch tactics. No more cattle wanderin' without hay in blizzards. Two years ago—winter-kill, thousan's of head dead, froze to death, starved."

"Don't seem logical to me," the Swede said. "Mike Western, now—he keeps the lid on, but I don't know how much longer. The woman—"

"What about the farm women?"

"They're talkin' fight—In the Woman's Club, my wife Hilda tells me. You don't know all the points, sher'ff."

"Has Powers—er one of his hands—done you farmers any wrong-doin's?"

"None thet I know of, sher'ff."

"Don't you think—if he didn't want you farmers—thet by now he'd have did somethin' about it?"

"You got a point there, sher'ff, but—"

"But what?"

The Swede had shrugged broad shoulders. "Nothin'. Fergit it, eh?"

Cal Sherman came out of the barbershop. "Had a

shave and a hair trim. Where in the town can a man buy a newspaper?"

"Two newspapers come into town once a week. That's when the only stage goes through. The Billings *Gazette* and the Great Falls *Tribune*."

"I mean the local newspaper."

"Oh, we ain't got one, now. Had a weekly—the Mad Horse Observer—until last Christmas, about the time Max lost his ear."

"What happened to the sheet?"

"Sheet?"

"Yeah, the newspaper."

"Oh, Mel Powers closed it down."

"Closed it down? Why?"

"Fat young Tarkington was publisher—owner. Mel ran him out of town. Tarkington was lucky Half Circle V hands didn't tar an' feathered him for what he printed."

"What'd he print?"

"Ran an editorial sayin' Mel an' his spread was holdin' back the town. Said one man ownin' all wasn't good. Smacked like William Jennings Bryan to Mel—thet Cross of Gold crap—an' Mel put the twins on him. The twins had jus' got here an' gone to work for Mel. An' Mel wanted to show the townspeople that his new hired guns was tough."

"Are they?"

"Brigham Tarkington found out they was."

"What do you think of them?"

"Don't rub me, Sherman. My poor ol' big butt still aches from the upendin' you guv me."

"You don't think with your butt, do you?"

Sheriff Ike Monday glared up at him, cheeks flushed with rage. His lips worked but no sound came and then he finally said, "No long spurs, cowboy. I've had a rough last few days. Four dead men, shot to ribbons, and who did it, an' for why?

"I understand. I'm damn' glad it isn't my job."

A wry thought ticked Cal Sherman. Here he'd killed three of the men and he was talking to the sheriff and the sheriff didn't know he was the killer. The main thing was to keep the sheriff in the dark, too.

That gold still bothered him. He'd seen Sheriff Hawkins lecturing his undersheriff and deputies.

Sheriff Hawkins didn't know what danger he was in. When that gold had slipped from his pocket he'd become a doomed man but he didn't know it.

Ignorance is bliss, Cal thought.

He hadn't heard all the details but to date he'd not heard of Powers demanding to know where the gold had come from had tumbled from Sheriff Hank Hawkins' shirt-pocket.

He figured that if Powers had not put the pressure on the pseudo sheriff, he'd soon tighten down the screws.

Not for one minute did Cal Sherman underestimate the inner cruelty of Mel Powers and his deadliness with his six-guns.

Powers would work on Sheriff Hawkins, sooner or later. No man was going to kill three Half Circle V hands and get away with it, Cal figured.

Cal and Sheriff Monday were headed for Mickie's saloon. "Powers'll fin' out where Hawkins got thet gold piece," the sheriff said.

"How?"

"Bullet dance, Sherman."

Cal had seen the bullet dance in operation. One man sneaked behind the victim, and disarmed him. Then the tormenters stood and shot at the victim's boots, making him dance.

"They make Hawkins dance, eh?" Cal said.

"They sure do. The twins an' Mel Powers. They've shot so close thet one time Hawkin's had nicks shot into the outside rims of his boot soles, they did."

It occurred to Cal that boot soles didn't have *inside rims,* but he kept that to himself. No use antagonizing this hidebound lawman. "What does Hawkins say when the dance is finished."

"He always swears he'll kill both Mel an' the twins. But he never does. Me an' Mickie always see thet his gun has no lead in its ca'tridges."

Cal remembered Sheriff Hank Hawkins' weapon. All it needed to be a lethal pice of killing material was shells with lead and powder in them.

Farmers rigs were at the saloon's hitch-rails. So were a number of saddle-horses. Cal read the Half Circle V on the broncs.

He and Sheriff Monday entered the saloon. Clouds of tobacco smoke assailed Cal's nostrils. He'd tried smoking—given it a good trial—but had then quit. That had been a number of years ago. He'd developed a cough in no time on Bull Durham. After quitting his cough had left. Now his lungs were his own and didn't belong to a Bull.

He wondered idly why so many Half Circle V men were in town and apparently on Mel Powers' payroll. This was the slack season between spring calf-gather and fall beef-roundup.

Usually after calf-branding ended a big outfit laid off hands until fall and beef-gather.

These unemployed hands then many times rode the grub-line until getting again on the payroll. That meant they rode from ranch to ranch and bummed grub and bunk until their welcomes wore out and they then moved on.

Some stayed on the home ranch and worked for only room and board until the payroll opened up again.

Cal instantly noticed all wore guns. That was odd. The average cowpoke nowadays usually was unarmed in town for most towns now had ordinances demanding a man toting a gun leave the gun at the sheriff or town-marshal's office. Evidently Mad Horse town had no such law.

Cal entered behind the sheriff, towering over the fat man. He might have been wrong but it seemed to him that the moment he entered a stiffness came over the group.

He thought at first he imagined this, but as he and the sheriff neared the long bar men parted and let them through, their eyes on Cal.

He was a newcomer. Four men this week had been shot and killed on this range. He was the only new man who'd ridden in. Naturally a certain amount of suspicion had fastened itself on his personage.

Also, he'd had a run-in with Mel Powers.

Mickie tended bar. Cal moved in beside the big woman.

"Not here to drink," he said quietly, "but here to work."

"Good. I need help. What drinks can you mix?"

Cal told her. Men watched.

"You know enough," Miss O'Hannigan said. "Mostly beer here. Lots of ice so don't go easy on it. Got an ice-house behind. Winter time come an' in some places the river freezes to the bottom."

Cal nodded.

"Want me aroun' for a while, Cal?"

"Whatever you want. Your bar, Miss O'Hannigan."

"I'll leave you alone. Hey, boys, our new bartender. Cal Sherman."

"Drinks are on the house," Cal said.

They began joking and kidding. The free drinks had loosened them a little.

"Free booze to the card tables, too?" the swamper asked.

Cal nodded. He glanced toward the gambling section at the end of the big room. Four tables there, but only one occupied.

He was surprised to see that a woman was the dealer. He remembered meeting her on the street an hour back.

He'd admired her womanly front. He'd mannishly glanced back and also had admired her womanly assets and small waist.

She was built as nicely as Bea Graham only where Bea's hair was massive red this woman had dark, sleek hair. Where Bea was light complexioned, this lovely was dark and mysterious.

Her eyes met his across the smoke-filled air. Their eyes held for a long moment and then she looked down at her chips and her deck of cards.

Cal found his heart beating faster. "What's the lady's name?"

"What lady?" the swamper countered. Cal told him. "Mary Malone."

Cal liked the name. A good solid name that fitted her. He pulled cold beer out of the ice-chest. He also tapped Great Falls beer out of the tap. The place seemed to lose its tightness.

He judged about every adult in town was in the bar. The town preacher sat in a back room with the town justice-of-the peace drinking where nobody could see him or his companion, the swamper told him on the quiet.

Three elderly town women were drinking alone against the far wall. Two were apparently getting rather drunk. They were loud and boisterous and called to the men at the bar.

"Why don't they go to the bar?" Cal asked.

"Town ordinance against women drinkin' standin' up," the swamper said.

Cal said, "Bullshit."

Cal figured he'd keep this job only a few days. He'd get to know these people a little better for he expected to live in this burg for some time, and he thought of the printing press and newsprint and type in the boarded up building.

He might homestead, too. Build up a nice, money-producing irrigated farm. He found himself wondering about who'd buy the Graham farm.

He'd look into that.

He then remembered that if anybody had seen him kill the three Mel Powers' gunmen, he was doomed. It would either be gunsmoke or his leaving town in the dark of the moon in a hell of a hurry.

He put these thoughts aside. Why cross a bridge before you came to it? And he was sure nobody had seen him.

A short man ordered a drink of whiskey.

"What'd you call it?" Cal asked.

The man repeated.

Cal said, "I never heard of that drink in my life."

The swamper tugged his sleeve. He and Cal moved out of the man's earshot. "He's pulled that afore, Mr. Sherman. Mickie's writed the igredients of thet drink on a piece of paper she's got pasted under the bar. Over there, Cal.''

Cal saw the instructions. He said to the man, ''Hell, I just remembered. I can make that drink.''

He mixed slowly and carefully, glancing down occasionally at his instructions. The drink was completed. The man tested it gingerly.

''Hit the spot,'' he said.

Cal glanced at Mary Malone. She happened at that moment to look his direction. He deliberately winked at her.

She didn't wink back.

Chapter Seven

Mickie O'Hannigan showed Cal his room upstairs. It was on the corner and had two windows so it had cross ventilation. "You'll need that these hot nights," the saloon keeper said.

Cal said, "I don't expect to tend bar long."

"Drifter, eh?"

"Not necessarily. I like Mad Horse Basin. Don't ask me why, but I do. It's nothing but sagebrush and dryness but just the same it has a great future, in my opinion."

"If more farmers come in, you mean?"

"That's the way I see it. With families and nice farms there'll be money and this town will take the place you say it has lost—and this time keep it, for good."

"I agree with you."

The saloon's swamper was a short, thin man of about fifty who limped badly, his left leg slightly shorter than his right, which then earned him the name of One Step.

One Step was from Arizona. Cal learned a horse had kicked him and broken his leg and a doctor had messed the leg up. Cal played his cards close. He didn't mention he, too, was from Arizona.

He learned things fast, that first shift.

He learned that when Mel Powers drank he became irritable, sullen, bitter. He became dangerous.

The twins drank cup for cup with their boss, each on Power's flank, each plainly guarding their employer.

Cal looked at Max's missing ear lobe. The thought came that after a man shot off your ear-lobe you sure as hell couldn't accept him as a friend. Apparently then only good wages kept Max—and his brother—close to Mel Powers.

Powers plainly wanted trouble with him, Cal soon realized. Cal wanted no trouble with Powers.

"Where'd you come from?" Powers demanded.

Cal looked at him. "Where we all come from. Our mother's wombs."

Somebody tittered. Powers shot a glance that direction, face flushed with anger. His eyes bored back to Cal.

"That's a smart-alec answer," he said.

Cal knew that if he showed any sign of backing down in front of the gun-toting cowman, Powers would dog him every minute on this drought-stricken range. He would have to be political, he decided.

"Smart alec question, Powers."

Cal had deliberately left out the *Mr.*

"Only man on horseback thet's come into town for some days," Powers said. "Farmers come in with wagons. Mebbeso you aim to take up a homestead?"

"I might."

"I can block you if I cares to—down at the land office in Billings."

"I haven't made up my mind yes or no yet on farming," Cal said.

Things were getting tight between Cal and the cowman. The twins had moved out cautiously another two feet from their gun-boss and their eyes were hard and strong against Cal Sherman.

Cal had hung up his gun and gun-harness when he'd gone to work. He was now happy he'd done so. He was unarmed and the code wouldn't permit his being shot unarmed.

"How long you expect to stick aroun'?" Mel Powers asked.

Cal shrugged. "Until I get wantin' to drift on."

Mel Powers opened his mouth and Cal figured the cowman was on the point of ordering him on when Sheriff Ike Monday tugged Powers' sleeve. "I'm out of booze, Mel."

Powers had been buying Monday drinks.

Powers snarled, "You're always out of drinks, Tinstar."

Cal saw the sheriff wince slightly. Plainly Monday didn't cotton to the label *tinstar*. A tinstar, Cal knew, was a blow-hard would-be lawman, such as he'd heard Wild Bill Hickcock had been.

The swamper at that moment tugged Cal's sleeve. "Miss Malone told me to tell you she wants to talk to you, Mr. Sherman."

Cal was surprised. What did he and the dark-haired beauty have to talk about? He looked toward Mary Malone's card table. She watched him.

He then understood. The swamper was adroitly removing him from Mel Powers' baleful presence.

"I'll talk to her," Cal said.

"I'll take over here."

Mary Malone had two elderly men at her draw-poker

table. Cal remembered seeing them around town. He bent over her. She had a nice perfume. She quietly said, "Mickie asked me to keep an eye on you and help you if necessary."

"I'll see it through."

"I'm here," the woman said. "Remember that, Mr. Sherman."

"I'll remember," Cal assured.

He returned to his job. He felt warm inside. It was good to have somebody on your side. He did not evade Mel Powers—and the gun-heavy twins—but he had no more words with them—and they sent none to him, for Sheriff Ike Monday kept Powers in conversation, and within an hour Powers and the twins left, the twins their proper distance and station ahead and behind the owner of huge Half Circle V.

By sheer accident Sheriff Hank Hawkins was entering the batwings when the trio left. The white-clad Powers grabbed for the green-clad pseudo sheriff. Hawkins leaped to one side, hand going to his holster. Powers' grasping fingers missed.

Sheriff Hawkins had his green-gripped pistol in his hand, barrel on Powers. Cal saw that he'd drawn very, very fast.

"You touch me, Mel Powers, an' I'll kill you!"

Powers laughed cynically. He suddenly reached out and before the youth could step back Powers had hold of the pistol. He wrenched it from the youth's grip.

He threw the gun toward the bar. It landed on the floor and slid to a stop, but no eyes were on it.

All eyes were on Hawkins and Powers and the twins.

"You're due for a bullet-dance, Sheriff."

Cal saw Hawkins' face pale. "No, no, Mel, please! Not that, my God, not that!"

The young man was shaking visibly. He was deadly afraid. His face was ashen, his mouth worked, his hands shook.

"Either that, or you tell me where you got that double eagle," Powers said.

Sheriff Hank Hawkins' spit-covered lips moved. At first, no words came—just a jumble of sound, nothing more. Finally his trembling lips formed words. "I don't know where it came from."

"It came from your shirt pocket, remember?"

"I remember. But how it got there, I don't know. I never saw it afore it falled from my pocket. I swear thet on the Bible, Mel, Who's got a Bible handy?"

Cal suddenly realized this town was torn into two camps. Plainly Mickie O'Hannigan was leader of one group—the opposition. Mel Powers and his powerful gundogs constituted the other faction.

"Ain't no Holy Book in this bunch of sots," a fat woman said. "We're akin with the devil, not the Lord." She spoke to Mel Powers. "Why not pick on somebody your own size, Mel?"

"Like who, fer instance?"

"Me."

"You got me outweighed," Mel Powers said. "You're in the heavyweight class, an' I'm jus' light-heavy."

That brought a bit of sullen laughter.

Powers spoke to Sheriff Hank Hawkins. "How in the hell would a gold piece get in your pocket without you knowin' it?"

"I don't know. Thet's the truth, Mel." Sheriff Hawkins was almost weeping. "But no bullet dance, god, no, Mel."

"There'll be no bullet dance with me around, son!"

The stern voice came from the top of the stairs. All eyes turned on heavy-set Mickie O'Hannigan standing there, her huge form encased by a formless blue dressing gown.

Cal saw relief flood the pseudo sheriff's face. Mickie came slowly downstairs, gown swishing. She picked up the young man's gun. She kicked open the cylinder and the cartridge cases flew clatteringly to the floor.

Cal noticed none carried lead.

Mickie handed the gun to the make-belief sheriff. She paid no attention to Mel Powers and his twin gundogs.

"Have you had anythin' to eat today, son?" She spoke to Sheriff Hawkins.

"Not since breakfast, mama."

Mickie looked at the swamper. "Take him back in the kitchen and cook up what he wants."

"My delight, Miss O'Hannigan."

The saloon-keeper still paid Half Circle V no attention. "If I hear another hard word down here—or a disturbance—I'm comin' down an' throwin' you all out and closin' the bar."

"Don't do that, please," a drunken female said.

That brought a laugh from everybody. This time the laugh was genuine. Mickie O'Hannigan turned. She climbed the stairs, not looking back; she disappeared.

Cal glanced at the doorway. It was empty. Mel Powers and his guns had disappeared, too.

But Cal saw them later through one of the windows. They walked tough and solid toward Half Circle V's office.

The others took up their drinking. Cal wondered where they got the money. One old man told him most were either on Half Circle V's pension system or on money borrowed from the big ranch until beef roundup came and a chance to repay.

"Mel don't like you, stranger," an old man told Cal.

"Maybe I don't like him, either," Cal said.

"Don't ask so many stupid questions, Smith," One Step growled. "This is a free country. A man can do what he likes as long as he wants an' if he don't harm other people, an' Cal's jus' here to tend bar."

"You don't say," the oldster said. "A lecture in the Constitution is next, One Step?"

"Screw you, Smith," One Step growled. He'd already picked up Sheriff Hawkins' cartridge cases. "Not a one with lead. Now why in the hell would Mel Powers be so all-fired interested in a mere twenty bucks when he's got a few thousan' an' is considered a rich man?"

"You got me," Cal said.

"An' where'd Hawkins get it?"

"You got me," Cal repeated.

"An' where'd them other double-eagles they've foun' aroun' town come from? I never heard of it rainin' gol'. Come to think of it, it ain't rained for months, either."

"Odd proceedings," Cal said.

"Sheriff Hawkins is in a bad position," One Step thoughtfully said. "He should be shipped outa here to Warm Springs but Mickie won't have none of it. She sure loves that boy."

"Maybe he's all she's got?"

"You said it, Mr. Sherman. She's had him since he was a small tyke, you know. Stage left him in her care years ago."

Cal nodded. "Heard of that, One Step."

"Anythin' you wanna learn about this town thet I know about I'll be glad to tell you, Mr. Sherman. You know, I kinda like you even though I don't know you very well—or for very long."

Cal glanced at him. The swamper's long whiskery face was serious. "How long has Miss Malone been in town?"

"Only a coupla months. Mebbeso not thet long. Let's say six weeks. Ain't much money here for a gambler but she said when she asked Mickie if she could run a table that she didn't want any more than a livin' outa her cards an' I reckon she's makin' that."

Cal remembered seeing a woman on horseback ride out of town toward the farm-settlements more than once during his three days hiding out on high Signal Butte.

His powerful field-glasses had shown she'd not been Miss Bea Graham. He'd then not known who the lady had been. Now he guessed it had been Mary Malone. "She know how to ride a horse?"

One Step glanced at him as he washed glasses, suds to his elbows. "Why'd you ask thet, Mr. Sherman?"

"Well, she looks like an Eastern girl to me, and most of them I understand don't ride horseback—only the rich ones."

"I don't know if she's from the east or not, but I do know she can set a horse—an' set one perfect."

"How come you know that?"

"They ain't much card playin' in the afternoon so about every day Miss Malone heads out on horseback. She's a good frien', they tell me, of that redheaded Graham girl—but shucks, Miss Graham's the only girl of any size an' age in thet nester group."

"She's sure a pretty woman."

"Which one you mean? Miss Malone or Miss Graham?"

Cal grinned. "Both."

"You can repeat thet without contradiction." One Step studied a glass' rim. "This is chipped a little. I'll lay it aside for the Montgomery family. They're poor people here. Lots of kids an' we give them all our chipped dinner ware, if it could be called such."

Mary Malone ran out of customers at eleven. There were still a few diehards perched close to the bar. She racked her chips and cards and pulled a canvas top over her table. The others were already topped. Apparently they'd been so for days for Cal had noticed dust on them.

"One short little beer, Mr. Sherman, and this girl upstairs and to her bunk."

"Tough day?" Cal asked.

She gave him a slanting glance. "Not as tough as yours, sir. You've had nothing that smacks of a picnic."

Cal poured a small cold beer. "I've seen worse, Miss Malone."

"Might I ask where?"

Cal almost told her of the hell on San Juan Hill. Cowboys with old army rifles—Civil War issue—on foot, bootheels digging, with the Spanish pouring down lead from new German Mausers. He caught himself in time. Let the public think what the newspapers had told them.

"Married life," Cal joked.

She looked at him. "I think you're joking, Mister Sherman, but I wouldn't know for sure. I've never been married."

"How'd a beautiful girl like you escape this far?" Cal asked, grinning.

"Guess nobody wanted me." She downed her beer neatly. "Another?" Cal asked.

"Not tonight. Goodnight."

"Goodnight, Miss Malone."

Cal watched her climb the stairs. She looked almost as pretty from behind as from the front. He had a young man's thoughts.

He glanced at the big wall clock. He noticed bullet-holes in the wall surrounding it. Evidently they'd not shot to hit the clock. They'd shot to see how close they could come to the timepiece.

One Step noticed his glance. "Mel Powers an' the twins," he said. "Mel came the closest. Less than one inch from the twelve o'clock number."

"Where'd he learn to shoot so good?"

"Danged if I know. They tell me he an' his pa got into a tiff a few years ago an' Mell pulled out. He came back after his pa died last winter, they tell me, an' all of a sudden he sure could handle a gun or rifle—put every bullet where he wanted it, an' danged fast, too."

The last customer—a wobbly-legged oldster—downed his suds, wiped his mustache, and tottered out, drunk to the gills. One Step moved in behind him and hurriedly closed the door.

He dropped a two-by-four length into the hooks to secure it. "I sleep close to the back door," he said. "On a cot there."

"What lights do we leave burning?"

"The lamp on the desk next to the door. Mickie leaves it there to tell anybody comin' late there's still a room upstairs."

Cal gave the saloon a final look. All glasses were washed, the beer tubs had ice, the bar was clean.

"Reckon that's it," he said. "Goodnight, friend.

" 'Night, Mr. Sherman."

Cal slowly climbed the stairs, boots in hand so he'd not make much noise. He swiftly reviewed the day. As

Mary Malone had said, it had not been a picnic. The haunting memory of four dead men still hung ghost-like over Mad Horse town and Mad Horse range.

He still wondered if hidden eyes had seen him kill the three Half Circle V toughs. That was a fear that all day had run through him now and then. He reasoned from a realistic point-of-view.

Had anybody seen him, surely that person would have reported to Sheriff Ike Monday—or Mel Powers—what he'd seen? And the report would have been made before this, of course.

And those damned gold pieces. . . .

He'd had compunctions when he'd taken them from the wallets of the three Half Circle V men he'd killed. It had been like stealing money, in one respect; in another, whoever would have searched the bodies would have taken the gold anyway, he suspected. He had just beat the second thief to the gold.

He should have studied the gold pieces more carefully. Then he'd been sure to have noticed the file-marks. He caught this thought and smiled. Who in heaven's name would suspect gold pieces marked?

He came to the head of the stairs. Before him stretched a carpeted hall with doors on either side. The door on his left was open. The room was dark. Mickie O'Hannigan's deep voice came from its darkness.

"That you, Cal?"

"Certainly is, Miss O'Hannigan."

"Can the Miss O'Hannigan crap, please—and just plain Mickie from here out, eh?"

"Suits me, Miss— I mean Mickie."

"Everythin' tip-top down below for tomorrow?"

"As clean as two men can make it, Mickie."

"Goodnight, Cal."

"Goodnight, Mickie."

Cal went down-hall to his room. Only one room showed lamplight under its door. This door was directly opposite his.

That would be Miss Malone's room. One Step had told him only two rooms upstairs—besides Mickie's—was occupied, the other occupant being the beautiful black-haired gambling lady.

"Time was when they almost fought for a room," One Step had mournfully stated. "Now—"

He'd spread his thin fingers significantly.

The night was hot. The two windows were wide open. Happily each had a screen or the room would have been filled with mosquitoes.

Naked, Cal lay on the sheet. He looked at the ceiling he couldn't see. Suddenly he smiled.

He'd not slept between sheets for a long, long time.

Chapter Eight

Next morning at ten, Smoky singlefooted north with a smaller buckskin gelding at his nigh-side, Cal Sherman slouched in Amarillo saddle, eyes on the Lone Wolf Mountains some six miles ahead.

He knew those mountains. He'd killed three men on their northern flank a few days ago.

Mary Malone said, "Your buckskin has a fast running-walk, Mr. Sherman."

"Cal," Cal reminded.

"Okay, Cal."

"Okay, Mary."

Mary Malone rode side-saddle, her voluminous split riding skirt draped over her saddle's fork. Cal had quickly noticed that she fitted a saddle well and rode well.

He also had realized he knew practically nothing about her. He'd noticed on first meeting her she'd worn no wedding ring, the second point he always looked at when meeting a good-looking young woman.

He'd been looking between the boards at the printing press and printing supplies left behind by the printer Mel Powers had run out of town when Mary Malone had ridden by, heading south toward the farm settlement.

He'd asked if he could ride with her. He didn't go to work in the bar until four that afternoon.

She'd said he could.

So he'd gone to the town livery and saddled Smoky who now pulled at the bit, full of ginger and oats and hay and again ready for the trail.

He covertly glanced at Mary Malone.

Mary's dark eyes were on the mountains ahead. Cal saw her profile, and he liked what he saw. He imagined her working at a wood-stove in a farmer's small house.

She'd fit in well, he figured. He wondered if she could milk a cow. Perched on a stool, head against the cow's flank, milk squirting into a bucket, the farm-cats sitting at a distance meowing for fresh milk.

She looked at him. He hurriedly looked away. He'd been having too many such family thoughts the last year or two, he realized.

He'd thought the same when he'd seen Bea Graham in town yesterday, too, he suddenly remembered.

"You were looking into that deserted print shop," Mary said. "And, for a woman's curiosity, may I ask why?"

"Always look in empty buildings," Cal said.

She looked away, He'd been a little abrupt. He realized he'd slightly offended her—or had he, for she said, "Curiosity killed a cat, I once heard."

"Quite a few things in that building," Cal said. "Printing press, newsprint, things like that."

"Newsprint?"

"Newsprint is rolls of paper you print on."

"You seem to know quite a bit about printing."

Cal hesitated, considered briefly, then said, "I was a printer's devil when just a little tyke in the fourth grade. Wouldn't be surprised if I still had printer's ink on my thumb, it's that hard to wash off."

He looked at his right thumb. She looked at the thumb, too. "Clean now," she said, and both laughed.

The ever-present Montana wind blew, and it was hell's oven hot. When they were a half-mile from the Graham farm the air suddenly became cooler, and Cal asked why.

"The wind is blowing across an irrigated field, but I hardly believe it is a field of the Graham family's."

Cal nodded.

"They're in too much of a tizzy to think about such a minor thing as irrigating. Bea was in town to see me this morning."

"I didn't see her."

"I believe you were in the barn currying your horse. She's going to work in the Mercantile, starting day after tomorrow."

"She's staying, then?"

"She is, but her mother and brother aren't. They're leaving tomorrow by wagon for Billings and the trail east to go back home again."

Cal didn't say it but he thought it was a good idea to get young Bill out of here. He'd heard that the youth was hotheaded and a few in the bar last night said they thought for sure the youth would have moved against whoever had killed his father—if he'd only known who had been the killer.

"Bea asked me to talk to her mother about selling the

homestead rights to me. I don't know how the deal can come about because they haven't lived on the land long enough, I understand, to fulfil all of Uncle Sam's homestead-requirements. You know anything about the Homestead Act?"

"Only that Abe Lincoln signed it during the Civil War."

"No more than that."

"A little more. A few years ago I had a friend who homestead in Nebraska. I went up from Texas with a cattle drive into Broken Arrow and I looked my friend up. He homestead on the Republican River out of Trenton, down just about where Nebraska joins Kansas and Colorado."

"I see."

"Chick had a bit of trouble, it seemed. So to help him I read up on the Homestead Act. If the Grahams haven't been long enough on the homestead to get their clear deed from Uncle I'm sure you can squat out the remainder of their time and get the deed just as they would of, had they stayed."

"That's what Mickie told me."

"I'm kind of interested in the Graham farm myself," Cal said. "Heard it was for sale."

"Goes to the highest bidder, I'd say."

"That's the correct way."

They were following the new wagon-road through sagebrush and across draws and hills. They were half-mile south of the farmsteads strung out in a chain along the base of the hills, each with a reservoir behind it in the coulee to store the precious rainwater and snow runoff.

They rode into a deep coulee whose bottom was thick and dark with high buckbrush, bullberry bushes, chokecherry trees and other timber, the drought having dried up the small stream of water that normally ran along its lowest point.

They were just about to this dry creek when a shot rang out to the south. Mary Malone's horse reared as she pulled in hurriedly. She glanced at Smoky, who stood rock still.

Smoky's saddle was empty, unoccupied stirrups swinging. The sudden bullet-report had surprised the girl. She seemed at a loss what to do. She hadn't seen Cal quit leather.

She noticed his rifle still rode in saddle-boot, though. She saw its stock sticking up over the buckskin's neck, just in front of the saddle. That meant Cal had not had time to snake out his rifle and take it with him.

Mary dropped her reins. She had control of herself now. Her voice was steady as she said, "No more shooting, please. We came on a peaceful mission, whoever you are."

There was no answer. She heard the sound made by a man approaching through the brush. Soon the farmer Mike Western came into view thirty feet away, rifle in hand.

Mike Western was unsteady on his laced-boots. Mary knew a drunk man when she saw one, and Western fitted her description.

"Scared yuh, eh?" Western leered. "Us farmers has guards out now. We ain't gonna git murdered like Si Graham was. Who was that gent with you? Whcrc t'hell did he go?"

"He's right behind you, Western!" Cal Sherman said angrily.

Western turned, a surprised look on his unshaven face. He turned just in time to hammer Cal's rising right fist with his blocky jaw. The fist won, Western went flailingly backwards.

His rifle flew from his grip. Cal picked it up and rapidly fired the remaining cartridges. Western's backward progress was rudely stopped by a big cottonwood tree.

Miraculously the tree above Western's head suddenly sprouted a handful of bullet holes. Western then realized Cal was emptying the rifle with the bullets whamming into the cottonwood about a foot above his head.

Mike Western opened his mouth. His tobacco-blackened fangs showed as he screamed, "Don't kill me, Sherman! For god's sake, don't kill me, man!"

Western slid down hurriedly. He sat at the tree's base. Cal Sherman let the firing-pin fall again. It clicked on an empty cylinder. He threw the gun to one side. He heard it land crashingly in the brush.

Mike Western felt of his mouth. He looked at the blood on his dirty fingers. "Cain't you take a joke, Sherman?"

"I can," Cal said. "But that was no joke."

"I'm kinda drunk," the farmer said.

"That's no excuse." He looked up at Mary Malone. "You all right, Miss Malone?"

"Just scared, that's all. I never saw you leave your horse."

"I never knew I left him until I hit the brush."

Cal Sherman spoke truth. Upon hearing the shot his actions had all been spontaneous. Without then realizing it the terror of San Juan Hill with the new German Mausers spouting down lead had been on him.

Weeks and weeks of practice with Bucky O'Neill's Rough Riders had come swooping in, demanding positive response.

She studied him. She seemed to be seeing him for the first time, or so it seemed to Cal, who had his eyes on the cowering Mike Western.

Western got up on shaky boots. He ran a dirty forefinger carefully around his upper teeth.

"Thought mebbeso you'd knocked a tooth or two outa me," the farmer said, "but it 'pears you didn't. If'n I tell what happened to Mel Powers he'll be almighty mad at you, bartender. An' when Mel's mad his two gunmen are mad, too."

"You working for Powers?" Cal asked.

"No, not in any sense of the word. But he wants us farmers in here to raise hay for him come winter time—an' he's right obstinate on thet point. He proved thet a few nights ago when Si Graham reared up at our meetin' an' done the same as called Mel Powers a liar, him claimin' that when we got our homesteads built up enough—an' when more settlers come in—Mel aims to take over our land and keep it for hisself."

"Do you believe Powers?" Mary asked.

"I do," the farmer said.

Cal tried something. "This isn't my business but seeing you shoot from ambush I've got a different opinion of you. They say you quarreled hard with Graham at the meeting."

"That's correct. I did. Graham had no right to get up an' insult Mel in front of all of us others when Mel an' the Twins had been good enough to come to our meetin' an' have Mel give his plans for betterin' this community—us an' him workin' together."

Cal nodded. "Some claim you and those three Half Circle V gunmen who they found dead rode out that morning to get rid of Si Graham for once and for always."

Western stared at him. "Who said thet damn' thing?"

"Talk around town," Cal said.

"They claim I kilt all three of them gun-dogs—Hersey, Snodgrass an' Martin? They sayin' thet?"

Alarm lifted the farmer's voice. When he hit the last word he'd been almost screaming.

Cal shrugged. "What I heard, that's all. Just thought I'd warn you, Western. People say one thing to a man's face. They say something totally different behind his back."

"I never rode out to kill Graham. Mind you, Mickie O'Hannigan said I was in a room upstairs all thet night, which I sure as hell was,"

Cal nodded. "She said if you'd gone past her door, even with your boots in your hands and not on your feet, she have heard you."

"That's right."

Cal swung into saddle. "Let me tell you something, Western. Last night I slept in the hotel."

"Done heared you had a room there. Go on."

"Well, I tested out the hearing of our friend Miss O'Hannigan. I passed her open door with her sleeping at four this morning and I didn't carry my boots—they were on my feet, along with my noisy spurs."

"She woke up fast, huh?"

Cal shook his head. "She didn't wake up at all. I even went downstairs as noisy as a man is when he goes down a stairs."

"An' thet still didn't wake her up?"

"Not an eyelash. I returned and there she was, sleeping and snoring. Which proves one thing, then, doesn't it?"

"Like what?" The farmer's voice was still too high-pitched.

"That you could have passed her door that night Graham and those three Powers' men got killed."

"I ain't no killer. I didn't have nothin' ag'in them three. Or Si, either, for that matter. What'd these people blame my killin' 'em on—that is, if I did kill 'em, which of course I didn't?"

"You got me," Cal said. "I never asked. I just decided to warn you, and don't ask my why. I don't know myself. Shall we ride on, Miss Malone?"

"Suits me," Mary Malone said.

They left the farmer behind gawking at them, one hand holding his aching jaw. When Cal looked back from the top of the grade he saw Western below in the brush searching for his rifle.

Mary said, "You sure can shoot. If Mel Powers got anything over you in the shooting line, it isn't much in my opinion. Where did you learn to shoot like that?"

"When I was married."

"Married? You tried that once before on me. It didn't fit then and it doesn't now."

Cal looked at her. Damn, she was a beauty! "You trying to tell me married people sometimes don't shoot at each other."

"Well, sometimes, yes. But—" Anger touched her high cheekbones. "I'm getting angry with you and I don't know for why!"

"What do you mean by that last?"

"I've just met you. You mean nothing in my life. I still don't believe you passed Mickie's door last night."

"I didn't."

"Then why did you say such a thing?"

Cal smiled. "Just to scare the bejeepers out of that ignorant farmer, that's why.

"You mean you instinctively disliked him?"

"You're right, Miss Mary Malone. Some pople when you meet them for the first time you instantly dislike. Others, you immediately like."

"Where would I fit in?"

"You, I instantly liked."

She looked at him. Her dark eyes danced. Was it laughter—or cynicism—behind them?

"I asked for that, Mister Sherman. I'll race you to the Graham farm,"

She hit her buckskin with her quirt. The little gelding leaped ahead on the dead run, dust spewing behind his shod hoofs.

Cal Sherman gave Smoky the spurs.

Chapter Nine

When Cal Sherman and Mary Malone rode into the yard of the Graham farm Cal was surprised to see the area filled with farmers. He'd been thinking over the incident with Mike Western and he now wondered if the farmer had not shot to kill him . . . and missed.

But why would Western lust to murder him?

He could think of no possible motivation, but he did figure that Western had deliberately taken to the bottle in search of courage. Past experience had shown him that man-killers kept their inner courage stoked by prime-proof alcohol.

He thought this was one moment, then reversed the next. Mike Western had been drinking, was drunk—had fired, and that was all. Or was it?

The thought came that perhaps Western had been hidden in the brush and had seen him kill Snodgrass, Hersey and Martin. That was an had been possible. But because of this, would Western want to murder him from bushwhack?

That theory was acceptable. Western could have been a very close friend to one of the dead men. He'd not reported what he's seen for two reasons, Cal figured.

Whom would he have reported to? Sheriff Ike Monday, for one? Cal quickly threw the obese, waddling lawman into discard. Monday had no power in Mad Horse town.

Actually, the fake sheriff, Sheriff Harry Hawkins, possibly commanded more power than did Sheriff Monday?

And if Western had seen Cal kill the three Half Circle V murderers, why hadn't he reported back to Mel Powers, who apparently had put two double-eagle gold pieces in the pockets of the dead gunmen?

Cal Sherman grinned ruthlessly. Western did not know he'd killed the three Half Circle V gunmen. Cal corrected that mental statement. If Western had seen his gun in action, Western had not reported such to Mel Powers, for was not Powers still searching for whoever had delivered those marked gold pieces across Mad Horse town?

But one point stood out, bleak and stark, and that was that his fist had not made him a friend of Mike Western, for sure. Western now had a grudge against him.

And he judged a man of Western's low intelligence would nurse that grudge, make it grow bigger and bigger until one day it would break out in hog anger, bringing with it gunsmoke and death.

He'd watch Western close from here out.

With this thought was a touch of dismay. He'd seen one of history's bloodiest battles down in Cuba. While it had been short, many men had died under gunfire. He wanted no more gunsmoke.

He had ridden into Mad Horse basin searching for a place to settle down, a place to work, a place to make a living. He would, in time, marry and have a wife and home, and eventually a few children.

By sheer accident, he'd started out on the wrong boot. He prayed silently that no human eye had seen him kill the three Half Circle V gunmen.

He had no compunctions, no regrets, that he'd been forced to kill them. If he'd not killed them, they'd have killed him. It was that simple. Luck and his fast gunspeed had made the difference.

Again he decided Western had not seen him. Hadn't Mickie O'Hannigan sworn that Western had spent the night in her hotel?

Therefore nobody apparently had seen the gunfight. He would never tell about it. That secret would go to the grave with him. The mystery of the four deaths—Graham, Hersey, Martin and Snodgrass—would never be solved, as far as he was concerned.

He put these thoughts out of mind. He rode into the gathering of farmers with one of Montana's most beautiful women riding beside his prancing buckskin, to be greeted by another Montana beauty.

For Bea Graham was that, and more. Her scarlet hair glistened under the hot summer sun. She wore a new housedress that did nothing to hide her womanly attractions.

"Lots of people here," Mary murmured to Bea.

"They came to see Mama and Bill off," Bea said, watching Cal help Mary dismount."

Hers were not the only eyes watching. Apparently every male in the group—married or single—watched the dark-haired gambler be set on the ground by Cal Sherman.

Bea gave Cal her hand. "Welcome, Mr. Sherman," she quietly said. "Will it be something hard or some lemonade?"

Cal looked inquiringly at Mary, for you gave the woman the floor first. Mary said, "A cold beer, maybe?"

"That we have. On ice. And you, Mr. Sherman?"

"Cal, please," Cal said.

Bea showed white teeth. "Then Cal and Bea it shall be."

"Lemonade," Cal said.

She led them to the table under the cottonwood tree. Cal looked about. Farmers had come on horseback and in rigs. Buggies, spring-wagons, buckboards, lumber-wagons.

He knew a few of the farmers from meeting them in town. They gave him nods, two lifted hands, but Cal sensed a stiffness in them—or was it only his imagination?

He looked at Bea, uncorking a beer bottle for Mary. She seemed to have bounced back fast from her father's murder.

Or had she?

Tomorrow morning she would watch a wagon roll out of this yard. That wagon could carry her mother and brother away. She would be alone in the world. She would have her memories.

A week ago her family had been complete. Her father, her mother, her younger brother, herself. Now an assassin's bullet had broken that family group forever. Never would it be bound together again.

Cal felt his heart go out to her. He talked to Mrs. Graham and Bill. Mrs. Graham said she was glad to go. She'd hated Montana since the first roll of a wagon-wheel into the Treasure State.

She'd welcome the midwest again.

Bill was taciturn, said little, but he would go with his mother, he had told his sister, and Bea thus told Cal. He had given up thoughts of revenge, for who was there to take revenge against?

Who had killed his father? Had it been Hersey, or had it been Martin, or had the killer been Herb Snodgrass? Nobody knew. His dead father couldn't tell. The dead three Half Circle V gunmen couldn't talk, either.

Maybe somebody still alive had been in on the gun-massacre, Bill had told Bea. But, if so, who had that person been, and where was he now? The truth might never come out. He would no longer nourish thoughts of death. He would remember his father as his father had been—slow-speaking, confident, loving his wife and two children.

Yes, Bill was ready to leave.

Bea and Mary were talking little woman-talk so Cal decided to walk around the farm and look things over.

The house wasn't much. No homestead shack ever was, Cal told himself. Usually a homesteader upon settling had little money, some with barely enough to pay Uncle Sam's filing-fees.

Most homesteaders were bachelors not by choice but by necessity—they could not afford a wife and family. Most knew little, if anything, about farming. Many were escapee Eastern factory workers who would toil no longer twelve hours a day for the other man but would gladly put in that great number of hours for themselves.

Cowmen in most cases definitely did not welcome them, for the cowman had long been the king of this range—and had run cattle gratis on land he did not own but which belonged to Uncle Sam.

But the day of the cowman was drawing to a close. Barbwire fences and windmills were moving west. The cowman had resisted in some incidents. Guns and gunsmoke had been called in.

Now Uncle Sam kept a more careful eye over his homesteaders, according to what Cal had read in the newspapers. Government troops, stationed on nearby army posts, could be called in at the first sign of trouble.

Most western territories—with the exception of New Mexico and Arizona—had also become stars in Uncle Sam's flag. That meant the arm of the law was closer now to each citizen.

When the States had been territories the law had been in Washington, D.C., but now it was in nearby State capitals. Montana's governor had the State National Guard at his command. He'd used it to forestall a couple of impending battles between diehard cowmen and farmers for his job was to protect all Montana citizens, not only the cowmen and their cowpunchers.

Perhaps Mel Powers had read the handwriting, Cal reasoned, for was he not stating he was in favor of the farmers to settle in Mad Horse and raise hay for Half Circle V's herds against deadly winterkill?

And had not Powers publicly stated he was getting rid of the old longhorn stock his father had trailed into Mad Horse after the Civil War? Had he not said he was shipping out his worthless longhorn bulls and shipping in beef-stock—Hereford, Shorthorn, Angus—to breed up his she-stuff and have them throw beef-calves, not skin and bone critters?

According to Mel Powers, Mad Horse Basin would see no strife between cowman and hoeman. But did

Powers speak the truth? While he'd tended bar only one night, Cal had heard the grumblings. Maybe Powers was just letting the farmers build up their storage reservoirs of irrigation water, change the sagebrush land into alfalfa fields—and when there were enough fields, he and his gunman would strike.

That appeared likely to Cal. He thought of the twins, gunhung and dangerous. And that Half Circle V cowpunchers all packed side-arms.

He decided the farm was too big to walk around in this hot sun. Graham had filed on the usual size homestead, one-hundred and sixty acres, which was a square, one-half mile on each side.

To walk around the farm would mean a man would walk four miles. Cal had a boot in stirrup when a nearby farmer said, "Did you meet Mike Wetern as you rode in, Mr. Sherman?"

Cal swung up. "I sure did. Down in a cottonwood grove."

"We posted him as guard."

Cal settled his length in saddle. "Why a guard?"

The man shrugged. He was middle-aged, bony, angular. Cal had heard his name in town but had forgotten it.

"Jus' thought it best, us farmers did."

Smoky played with the roller in the port of his curb bit. "I still fail to understand."

"Well, four men got killed less than a week ago. The killer might still be around, you know."

"Maybe the four fought among themselves? And each of them killed the other?"

"Could be. Logical. You aim to stay in Mad Horse?"

Cal had heard this question too many times. He turned Smoky with, "You aim to stay?"

He loped away.

He rode first south toward the reservoir. The small dam was made of dirt with a rock face. Fresnos and slips had pulled the dirt from the face of the hills beyond the dam.

The drain-gate was deep in the dam so every possible drop of water could eventually be drained. It opened and closed by a steel-gate. Thus water was allowed into the main ditch.

The gate was closed. Only a dampness of water seeped through the barrier. The water level in the dam was low. Cal figured the reservoir less than one-third full.

This range—and this dam—needed water.

The spillway was made of rock and concrete. When the dam was filled the surplus water ran free over the spillway into the main ditch. This was the safety-valve that would keep the dam from washing out from too much water.

Graham had eighty acres under cultivation. Cal figurted sixty acres of this were in alfalfa. The field had just been mowed and raked and the alfalfa already stacked.

Cal was no judge but he figured the cutting had netted around fifty tons. Another older stack, now slightly brown from the sun, was beside the newer stack.

This told him the brown stack contained the hay from the first cutting. He'd read where if there was rain and the summer was long enough a farmer could get three crops a year from alfalfa.

Graham had already got his second.

The bottom half of the homestead had not been plowed. It was in natural sagebrush and bluejoint grass. Had it not been irrigated, the grass would now be dead and brown.

But it was not dead and brown. It was sparkling green and high as the knees of a tall horse. Cal dismounted. He slipped the bit from Smoky's mouth. The big buckskin began immediately grazing, tearing the tall grass into him by tough stained teeth.

Cal Sherman looked about.

Once again the beauty of Mad Horse Basin struck him. He looked north across the basin with its tree-lined river toward the magnificent Highwoods, miles away and blue and mystic, the higher peaks with their glaciers and snow white and calm and majestic against blue space.

He looked west.

There other mountains met his eye. They were more peaked, more snow-covered, than the Highwoods. A rougher mountain range. Dark with pine and spruce, they bulked huge and ponderous and boulder-strewn, a natural guard blocking the basin's western flank.

East the plains of Montana ran on and on, broken by red slashes of badland gulches, formidable and without hope—for only salt-weed and gumbo-weeds grew on the badlands' scraggly hills white with alkali and eroded by millions of years of rain and run-off snow water.

This land would forever be without value. Nothing commercial would ever be grown there. True, coal was close to the surface; in many places, it shoved its black shoulders free and visible to the eye.

Here the redskin had found the red and white and other colors with which he had decorated his fighting-face during his savage combat with other tribes, and the final showdown against his white enemies. Here, too, he had chipped loose lignite coal to heat his buffalo-hide lodge when blizzards swept across this northern land, howling and far below the freezing point.

He looked south. And then, he saw the four riders

heading his direction. He recognized three of them immediately.

And the sight of them froze his blood in his veins despite the over hundred degree summer heat.

Now what the hell was this?

Chapter Ten

The three riders were not riding abreast. One on a black horse rode slightly ahead and to the right of the middle rider, a man in snow-white suit who rode a gray horse.

The rider on this man's left rode a pace behind. He was dressed in black as was the lead rider; he, too, had a black saddle cinched onto a black gelding. He plunged forward, black on a run.

Dust swirled upward, almost hiding the fourth rider. He rode ten paces behind the man on the big gray horse. He rode a black and gray pinto that Cal remembered glimpsing back in the buckbrush a few minutes ago.

For some reason, Cal's right hand automatically landed on his holstered gun. He then caught himself and removed his hand.

As they neared, the nigh-rider in black pulled back the necessary paces, and allowed his leader to come on ahead.

Mel Powers pulled his black to a dust-jarring halt, the twins following suit, the man on the pinto also reining in. For a moment dust swirled around Cal Sherman, standing there, and then the wind shipped in, scattering the dust and clarifying the scene.

Cal looked up at Mel Powers. "Something bothering you, Powers?"

Mel Powers looked at him. Cal glanced at the twins. He located the one with the missing ear-lobe. He was Max. He rode nigh front. Ted rode off-back. They'd pulled in three paces behind their boss. The pinto and rider were behind them.

Cal looked back at Mel Powers.

Powers said clearly, "How come you ride down to this part of the Graham ranch?" He didn't await an answer. "If you have any ideas of buyin' the spread, discard them here an' now an' this minute, Sherman."

"What makes you think I want to buy it?"

"If you didn't, why are you down here lookin' it over?"

Cal said, "If I wanted to buy it, would it be any of your business, Powers?"

"It would be."

"In what way?"

"When enough farmers come in—and enough land is in hay fields—I intend to buy each one out."

"With what, for instance. Not gunsmoke, huh?" Cal then wished he'd not said the last sentence. His anger at this rude and crude affair had gotten the better of his logic and tongue.

Mel Powers laughed shortly. "You been readin' too many of them western stories, Sherman. The day of guns on open range is past. A cowman can't buck Uncle Sam and his laws. You're talkin' through your hat, man."

"Okay," Cal said, "We'll let that ride." He looked

significantly at Max. Max's black-holstered black-gripped pistol was tied to his flat thigh. Cal looked at Ted. Ted's gun—also black-butted—was also thonged down. He looked back at Mel Powers' holsters.

He'd noticed one thing, fast. Sometimes each of the three packed two guns. Sometimes they packed but one. He spoke to Mel Powers. "You don't want me as a farmer, eh?"

"I definitely do not."

"Why?"

"You ain't no farmer. You ain't no gambler. Jus' now you're tendin' bar, but you sure as hell ain't no bartender. You don't fit in anywhere, Sherman. So I'm askin' you—jus' what the hell is your deal in this basin an' town?"

Cal spoke clearly. "And for another time, I'm telling you the same thing, Powers. You can kiss my ass."

Max cut in with, "You can't talk to Mr. Powers like that,"

Cal looked the gunman's direction. "I can't?" he said. "You seem to forget one thing, lead ear."

"Lead Ear, eh? And what'd I forget?"

"That I just talked to him in the manner you said shouldn't be done." Cal watched the gunman carefully. "I just told him to kiss my ass, remember?"

"You can't—"

"That's enough, Max," Mel Powers snarled.

Max looked at his identical twin. Ted shrugged. Mel Powers did not see the gesture. Max clipped shut his mouth.

Cal Sherman realized he was in a precarious position. He faced three fast gunmen. They could kill him where he stood. He might get one but if he did he'd be lucky—very, very lucky.

He decided to under no circumstances allow his hand to wander close to holstered gun.

He glanced at Mike Western. What was Western doing with these gunmen? His question was soon answered by Mel Powers.

"Western, ride even with me."

Western moved his pinto ahead, reined in. He had baleful, ugly eyes for Cal Sherman.

"This man for no reason beat you up, Western?" Mel Powers spoke without giving the farmer a sidewise glance.

"That he did, Mr. Powers."

Cal spoke to Western. "For no reason, Western?"

"For no reason," Western said.

Cal spoke to Powers. "Your farmer friend is a lying sonofabitch. Miss Malone and I rode the wagon-road into a gully. He cut down on me with a rifle. Whether he aimed to kill and miss—or shoot to warn—I don't know. But I worked him over."

"He didn't call out he was on guard?" Powers asked.

"He certainly did not."

Powers spoke to Western. He still did not look at the farmer. He kept his dark eyes on Cal Sherman.

"Did you or did you not warn Sherman?" Powers asked.

"I—"

"You what?" Powers insisted.

"I might have. I might not have. I forgot. A man can't remember everything, you know."

Powers spoke to Cal. "He seemed undecided. Usually when people hem and haw they are lying. I speak to you. Did he warn you?"

"He did not," Cal said.

Powers spoke to Max. "You and Ted give him a

treatment for lying, eh?''

Max whirled his black horse. ''With pleasure.'' He spurred back of Powers, unbuckling his catch-rope. His brother came in on the opposite side, also taking down his hardtwist catch-rope.

Western tried to turn his pinto to flee. The pinto was not fast enough. On each side sudenly a big black horse penned in the smaller paint. The catchropes lifted, poised—then fell.

And they fell with savage, cutting power. Cal noticed right off that each rope was a Mexican maguey lasso. A maguey made a fine small rope for frontfooting and light roping. Heavy roping would break it. It also was very stiff and when it hit human flesh, it most times cut.

Mike Western screamed. He covered his head with his forearms. Ropes beat down his arms.

Ropes smashed across his unshaven face. Blood leaped.

The beating occurred behind Powers. Powers did not even glance at the unfair thing behind him.

Powers spoke to Cal. ''I was goin' buy this farm for Western.''

Cal had no answer.

''I hate a liar,'' Powers said.

Cal looked beyond the beating. Two riders had just left the Graham homestead buildings, a half-mile away.

They were headed this direction. They rode fast. Dust hung behind them, wind whipping it.

The distance was too far for recognition. Cal looked back at Powers. The young cowman seemed amused at some inner thought. A rough smile broke his wind-cracked lips.

''I wonder if ever there has been a politician who is not also a liar?'' Powers made it a question.

"I hardly think so," Cal Sherman replied. "I think the prime requisite of being a politician is the ability to lie—and with a straight face."

"And to steal successfully, too," Powers said.

Cal watched the riders. He still couldn't identify them. One thing was sure—they were really pounding horseflesh.

Western was now on the ground. The twins had uncoiled their maguey ropes. They snapped the raw ends at the farmer. They were experts. The lasso-ends were stripping the flannel shirt from the farmer who lay on his belly, head buried in his arms.

Powers continued on, voice dead. "They tell me you've been lookin' between the cracks into the vacant buildin's in town, Sherman. The kids been watchin' you on the sly. They always report back to me, you know. A few nickels, no more, no less."

Cal studied the cowman. Once again he wondered if Mel Powers possessed all his mental powers. This beating of Western only because Western lied did not ring true.

Not to Cal Sherman, anyway. . . .

He's supposed to be a friend of the farmers, but here he is having his gunmen beat the hell out of a farmer, which to me don't make sense. . . .

Surely the other farmers would side with Western? Or would they? Cal realized he did not know the true temper of this farmer-group. He'd not been on this range long enough.

All he knew was what he'd learned one shift at bartending. Maybe these farmers were not in accord with Powers? He then remembered hearing about the meeting a few nights ago—the night before the murder of Si Graham.

From what he'd heard, only one farmer had stated he had had no trust in Half Circle V. And that farmer had been Graham.

And Graham, next morning, had paid with his life for his statements. . . .

Cal spoke to Powers. "Your two men might kill Western. They've cut him up pretty bad."

Powers spoke without turning in saddle. "That'll be enough, Max. No more, Ted."

The lassos stopped hammering, cutting, bringing blood. The twins began coiling their ropes.

Ted said quietly, "Two riders comin', boss."

Powers' eyes were on Cal. "Who are they?"

"Two females."

Powers still did not look backwards. "I asked you their identity, not if they were male or female."

"Miss Mary Malone. An' Miss Beatrice Graham."

"I thank you, Ted," Powers said.

Cal swung into saddle. Mary and Bea had slowed down to a long trot. They reined in and both girls looked at Western, groaning and still on his belly, and Mary spoke to Cal.

"What happened, Cal?"

Cal said, "I'll tell you later, please."

Mel Powers said, "Good afternoon, ladies." He spoke to Cal. "Thanks for the nice talk, Mr. Sherman."

"Very nice talk, indeed." Cal was cynical.

Powers overlooked the cynicism. He spoke to the twins. "I reckon we'd best get back to the gatherin'."

The twins turned their blacks, Power's big gray following suit. Suddenly Powers reined in, the twins riding on.

Powers spoke to Mary Malone. "Mr. Sherman told me that Mr. Western shot at you two when you rode through Hangman's Coulee."

"He did," Mary said.

"I have just one question to ask you, Miss Malone. Before firing did Mr. Western give you a cry of warning, or didn't he?"

"He never warned us. First thing we knew, a shot whistled overhead—and Mr. Western fired it."

Powers' touched his flat-brimmed white hat. "That is all I wish to know. Again, good afternoon, ladies."

The twins already loped south. Powers touched his star-roweled spurs to his gray.

The grain-fed big horse leaped ahead. Soon it was even with the twins who quickly assumed their correct positions—one a pace ahead and a few paces to the right, the other a pace behind and proper distance.

Bea Graham frowned. "Now what was this all about?" She referred to Western, still on his belly, and moaning softly.

Cal hurriedly told her.

Mary went to Western. "They're gone now," she told the prone man. She spoke to Cal. "And Powers had the twins beat him with their ropes because Powers took your word over his?"

"That sounds loco," Cal said. "But it's the truth. And while they were hammering Western Powers gave me a discourse on the dishonesty of a politician, and such things."

Bea studied him. "Have you gone loco, Cal Sherman?"

Cal had to smile. "No, that's the truth." He looked at Mike Western. "I guess our gunman has decided to sit up."

Western sat in a stupid slouch. His face was not cut as badly as Cal had first thought. "I think the man is crazy," Western said.

Bea said, "Maybe you had it coming?"

Western wiped his face with a red bandana. "Don't get flip with me, Miss High an' Mighty Graham! I was posted in thet coulee to see no strangers come in to disturb the farewell party for your ma."

"I can't find a farmer who posted you," Mary Malone said, "and while you were down there, I asked around."

"I don't want to talk to a woman," Western said. "You start argufyin' about one thing an' you end up argufyin' about somethin' miles an' miles away."

"I thank you," Bea Graham said sarcastically.

Western said no more. He strode to his horse, swung up into saddle, turned the horse pointing east, and loped away, evidently leaving the farewell party behind.

"Where's he headed for?" Cal asked.

Bea answered. "Heading for his homestead, I guess. Dad put a gate in the lower northeast corner. He can get out that."

"I don't understand all this," Mary said.

Cal said, "I sure don't, either. Nobody supposedly posted him as a guard, you've learned." He spoke to Mary Malone.

"That's right."

"So Powers said he had originally wanted to buy this homestead for Western," Bea said. "The gall of the man. He never contacted Ma or Bill or me at any time."

"Can you sell your homestead rights?" Cal asked.

"I really don't know. We haven't been here long enough to have final papers," Bea explained.

"I'm sure you can sell," Mary said.

"Sell what?" Bea asked.

Cal said, "Your first papers. The homestead entry will just pass from your father's name to the new buyer and he is then commissioned to stay and improve the land. And when final papers are given, he will receive them."

Bea looked at Cal. "You seem to know a lot about homestead laws."

"I've studied them rather carefully.

"You intend to homestead?" Bea asked.

"I might. I might not." Cal turned his horse toward the farewell party, the girls mounted and riding one on each side.

Mary said, "I've been thinking about Powers having the twins whip Western."

Cal and Bea looked at her.

"Mickie says Western spent the night—the night of the killing—in his room at the hotel. She claims nobody could walk past her open door without her coming awake."

Cal said nothing.

Bea also was silent.

"Well, maybe Western did get past her? And maybe he got out there in the hills and maybe he killed all those people?"

"I've thought of that," Bea said, "but I've never told anybody, 'cause I can't for my life see a reason for Western doing that."

"He quarreled with your father, I've heard," Mary explained.

"Yes, that is true. They had a few hot words. Western was drinking, as usual—but still, I can't imagine Mike Western as a cold blooded killer."

"Those dead Half Circle V men, too," Mary said.

Cal had no words. This was ironic, in a sense. Here he, the true killer, rode with these two young women while they discussed who had killed and why he had killed the three Powers' cowpokes.

Cowpokes? Cal corrected that. *Gunhung, hired killers, not cowpokes. Those gold pieces, remember?*

Mary said, "My theory doesn't hold water. Sorry I said it, folks."

"Please none of us report this to Bill," Bea said. "He'd never leave with Mama, then!"

"I'll say nothing," Mary said.

Cal said, "That goes for me, too, Bea."

They rode a distance without speaking, hoofs making plopping sounds on the dry earth. Finally Cal said, "I think it best we say nothing about this to nobody, and leave it all in Western's hands. If we tell the farmers will be up in arms, and God knows what would happen next."

Both women agreed. Both pledged themselves to silence.

"How come you girls rode out to me?" Cal asked.

Bea said, "Mary thought of it."

Cal looked at Mary.

"Well, Powers and the twins rode in. They saw you in the pasture and asked who that rider was and somebody said, 'Cal Sherman,' and they turned their horses and rode down on you, Western trailing."

Cal frowned. "Why would that make anybody suspicious?"

"Western was the one," Mary said. "After you'd whipped him—and him riding with Powers and those two gunmen—"

Cal nodded. "I understand. And thanks." He hesitated, then said, "You know, they could have killed me. Each could have said afterwards I drew first, and I was killed in self defense."

Bea said, "Why would they want to kill you?"

"I haven't the slightest idea," Cal said, "except

Powers when he called me in the school house meeting acted like he just hated me on sight—and needed no further motivation."

"You're a mystery on this range," Bea informed. "Everybody wonders where you came from and why you are here, especially you coming in so soon after my father and those three were killed—or killed themselves, or whatever happened out there."

"I reckon you're right," Cal thoughtfully said.

Chapter Eleven

When Cal and the two women returned to the farewell party Mel Powers and the twins had left and soon Sheriff Hank Hawkins and his under-sheriff and deputies rode in, resplendent in all green even to boots and gun-grips. Cal wondered where they got the money for such new outfits.

"Mickie," Mary told him. "They worked for her—cleaning the yard, her barn, painting inside the saloon—Mickie O'Hannigan, I have heard, is a very wealthy woman."

"I would judge so," Cal said.

Mary glanced at him. "She's got a case on you. She told me so."

Cal looked at her. Apparently she spoke the truth. "She's going to be disappointed. She's too old and I'm too young to marry."

"You better watch her," Bea said.

"Rawhiding is the word," Cal said and added soberly, "Not the kind those twins handed Western, either."

None of the farmers knew about the beating. Cal and the three girls decided to keep it secret. As Cal said, "Let Western tell them the details. Me, I've got enough trouble without looking for more."

Sheriff Hank Hawkins and office staff were soon followed by the real sheriff and One Step. "Sheriff saw Hank leave town," One Step told Cal, "an' he darned well figgered somethin' might take place out here so he trailed along an' Mickie saw him leave an' tol' me to ride out an' see what would happen."

Cal told about Mel Powers and the twins just leaving.

"Saw them three off to the west," One Step said. "Seems like one of the town kids tol' Mel jus' this mornin' that he'd been on Signal Butte an' it looked to him like somebody had done made a camp up there for a couple of days, at least—judgin' from the age of the horse droppin's an' fire ashes an' such."

"The day of the wandering redskin is past," Cal reminded.

"One Step scratched his bald dome. "Mebbeso Cal an' the twins ain't climbin' Signal in this heat but Mel keeps an eye on every stranger what rides in on his range."

"That's no understatement."

Let Half Circle V search the top of Signal Butte . . . I left no tell-tale prints there . . . I saw to that . . . And nobody saw me ride away from the Butte . . . I scouted damned good and thorough before leaving to make sure no riders were in the area. . . .

Sheriff Ike Monday waddled up. Sweat covered his beefy face. "Thet damn' would-be sheriff's causin' me a pack of trouble. . . . Thet big woman down there in the basin bosses me aroun' like she an' me was man an' wife!"

Cal hid his grin.

"Damn' if I know what the hell is goin' on on this grass," the sheriff said, "but somethin' big is in the wind—an' don't ask me where or why or when, 'cause I damn' don't know myself." He glanced at Bea and Mary. " 'Scuse me, ladies, fer bein' foul-mouthed."

"We both know how to cuss," Bea said.

Mary said, "And curse loud and profane, too, sheriff."

Cal dug out his Ingersoll. "Time I head down-hill and go to work, people. You riding back with me, Miss Mary?"

"Just as soon as I say goodby to Mrs. Graham and Bill."

Cal also bade the mother and son farewell. Soon he and Mary were heading north toward Mad Horse town, down there in the cottonwood trees along the river.

A mile from town the clatter of running horses reached them. Soon Sheriff Hank Hawkins and his office-staff thundered past, six-guns raised as they spurred through the dust.

"Sonsofbitches held up the bank," Sheriff Hawkins screamed as he streaked by. "Killed the cashier, got off with fifty thousand bucks. Headed north but we aim to cut them off at the pass, for sure."

"Which bank?" Cal hollered.

"First National. Timbuktu."

The posse thundered by, dust rising high behind. Mary and Cal held in their mounts to let the dust blow away.

"Wonder if he knows where Timbuktu is located?" Mary asked.

"I hope so. I sure don't know."

Mary laughed. "Neither do I."

Cal liked her. She was good company. She and he fitted in together easily, naturally liking the other.

Or was she just easy to get along with? He only been around red-headed Bea Graham a few times but they seemed like old-time friends, too. Cal hid an amused grin. Well, anyway, it was interesting. . . .

Mel Powers and the twins were not in town when he and the lady-gambler entered. Mary learned that from a tow-headed boy of about eleven. "Somebody said they done rode east of town to the region aroun' Signal Butte."

"Thanks, Jimmy."

Cal was pressed for time. He hurriedly washed his hands and dusted off his clothing and tied a bar-apron around his middle. Mickie threw her apron aside and said, "Anythin' important happen out in the hills, Cal?"

"Nothing to speak of. Just another goodby party."

Sheriff Hank Hawkins swaggered in, accompanied by his under-sheriff. He brushed dust from his green finery. "Well, we got the bastards, Mr. Sherman. All the gold, too, down to the last five dollars. We hung 'em high an' left their corpses hangin' by the necks to warn off other fools who think they can pull off a robbery in my territory."

"That's the way a lawman has to do it," Cal said.

Mickie spoke to Cal. "What's he talkin' about?"

Cal told her about the Timbuktu holdup. "Shaw, now, he's run down another bunch of bank-robbers, eh? That makes three bank robberies this week, if memory is right. What'll it be for you and your deputy, son?"

"Undersheriff, not deputy. Whiskey straight for me."

"Me, too," the undersheriff said.

Mickie took a quart of Old Saddle Maker from the back-bar. She poured fizzling drinks into two steins. Cal didn't know what was in the bottle but he knew it was nothing alcoholic. She'd concocted this drink herself and had told him that to her and her adopted son it was called 'whiskey straight."

Sheriff Hawkins and his undersheriff seemed content with the drink. They repaired to an empty card table and began drinking and conversing in a low voice.

Cal wondered if they were not plotting another campaign against crime. "Their short-arms are the real thing," he told Mickie.

"I know that. I make sure they have only blanks." She glanced at him. "You used the word *short arms.* That's an army term. Only one I've heard use it was my father and he was a veteran under Jeb Stuart."

"Reckon I got it from my father, too," Cal fibbed. "He was under Grant." He had no desire to discuss San Juan Hill.

"Got to do my bookkeepin'." Mickie started climbing the stairs. Cal had the bar to himself. Only Sheriff Hawkins and his undersheriff were in the place.

Mary was upstairs. She'd told him afternoons were always dull except on Saturday. The bar was closed until six on Sundays.

Cal began dusting off back-bar bottles. He'd never imagined a bartender had so many things to do. He definitely did not like bar-tending. The experience was a good one. He'd discovered a trade he really disliked.

But the job had a purpose. He was looking over Mad Horse town and this job gave him an inside ear for the bar was the center of the town's gossip, he'd learned.

"That dustin' ain't your job, Mr. Sherman," Sheriff Hank Hawkins said. "That's supposed to be did by ol' One Step."

"But One Step isn't here." Cal belched loudly. He'd

taken a few slugs of Montana Lightning at the farewell party and it still didn't sit well.

"I'll rake One Step over the coals when he comes in," Sheriff Hawkins said.

"Thanks, Sheriff."

"You like my Ma, Mister Sherman?"

Cal mopped the barn. "A very admirable lady, Sheriff."

"She loves me an' I love her. When nobody wanted me—when I was a baby—she took me in—"

"So I've heard," Cal said.

"She raised me to be what I am today—the lawman of Mad Horse County," Sheriff Hawkins said.

Cal nodded.

"Any man lay a hand on my Ma, an' he's me to tend with," Sheriff Hawkins informed.

"The Sheriff speaks true," the undersheriff said.

"I doubt him not a bit," Cal informed.

Sheriff Hawkins said, "Man touch Ma with hate in his system, an' kill him in his boots I will do, Mr. Sherman."

"I doubt you not a bit," Cal said.

The undersheriff said, "You won't see ol' One Step for a day or so. He was boozin' thet moonshine them farmers make. You take a snort of it, Mr. Sherman?"

"Three of them," Cal said, "and my life—and belly—will never be the same. The farmers got stills?"

"Two got coils," Sheriff Hawkins solemnly stated. "Isaac Malone an' Louis Newberger. Ag'in the law, those stills."

Cal said nothing.

"I should close 'em down," Sheriff Hawkins said. "Contrary to both state an' Uncle Sam's laws, them stills. Pay no state or federal taxes. Clear violation of state and United States' liquor laws."

"His Ma sent Monday out there twice to close them stills," the undersheriff said.

Sheriff Hawkins eyed his subordinate coldly. "I'm tellin' this, not you. Never usurp your superior's power. If you do once more, out you go—your wages in your pocket, sir."

"I forgot, Sheriff."

Sheriff Hawkins spoke to Cal. "Monday got drunk. Both times, he got pickled. Even with his bum belly, he drunk that lightnin'. Stayed out with them farmers about a week, drunk to the gills."

"You think One Step'll do the same?" Cal asked.

"He'll be good for two days, no more. Then he'll sleep it off an' lag his rump aroun' for a few days an' then he'll straighten up for about six months, an' then the moon'll be full one night an' he'll start howlin' again for a few days."

Cal was glad the undersheriff had got the sheriff off the killing-idea. Men with the low mentality of Sheriff Hawkins were liable to just get excited and grab a gun and start shooting the first direction that came to their minds. They were dangerous, Cal well knew.

"Your ma believe in the full moon and things like that, Sheriff?" Cal asked.

"She sure does. When the moon is full this bar has more customer. There's fightin' an' boozin' an' a all-around good time. Me an' my men have their hands full come a full moon, believe you me, Mr. Sherman."

"Tell Mr. Sherman about Easter, Sheriff?" the undersheriff suggested.

"Oh, last Easter. Full moon, you know. Always is on Easter. Man alive, did Ma rake in the dough. Vistin' preacher for a revival. Him an' our preacher got so drunk the tent had no pastor for three nights runnin'."

"What'd the people do for a minister?" Cal asked.

"Sheriff Monday—that phony—doubled in. He can preach a little an' he's got callouses on his knees, you know. Big fake. I should sent a bullet through his big gut one of these fine evenings."

There he is, back on the killing angle again, Cal thought. He wished somebody would come in. He was weary of talking to these two loonies. This burg definitely had too many lawmen.

And both, in his reckoning, were incompetent.

"Powers ever find out where you got that gold piece?" Cal asked.

"Ain't questioned me again. Hell, I don't know where I got it, myself, an' I speak the gospel truth, Mr. Sherman."

"He really don't know," the undersheriff affirmed.

"I asked Ma if the stars could tell her where it come from. She talks to the stars a lot, you know—knows just where each one is each minute of the day, an' when one crosses t'other, or somethin' like that, things happen an' she can foretell, like them gypsy ladies in them carnivals thet visit here about once a year."

"Ma's a great astronomer," the undersheriff said.

Sheriff Hawkins said, "Astrologer, not astronomer."

"And the stars haven't told her?" Cal asked.

"Not a word. Where thet gold come from is a mystery to all. An' why Powers is so all-fired interested in it nobody kin understand."

"Just like one of those mystery stories," Cal Sherman said.

The undersheriff idly said, "Mebeso Mel'll make you bullet-dance again, Sheriff?"

He then clamped a hand to his mouth. He'd said the

wrong thing. But it was too late to retract.

The effect on Sheriff Hank Hawkins was astounding. One moment he was normal, face calm and grave and the next, he was completely different.

His face turned chalk-white. His bottom lip trembled. His eyes bugged out like glass marbles.

He started to stand. He couldn't make it. He got halfways up, then was momentarily frozen. He stared ahead at nothing. His hand went for his right-hand gun.

The hand missed the gun's handle. It went down his side, fingers clutching. The youth bent almost double. He still couldn't rise. He seemed caught in a vise bending him double.

Cal started around the bar. The undersheriff waved him away. Cal stopped. He watched.

"He'll get over it soon," the undersheriff said. "I shouldn't have mentioned the bullet dance. I plum forgot, Mr. Sherman."

Cal had no words. He watched Sheriff Hawkins. His heart pounded dully. Sympathy ran out of him toward the unfortunate youth.

He'd seen a youth go through a similar spasm in the Rough Riders. Bucky O'Neill had afterwards asked if the youth had wanted to go home. He'd be honorably discharged, big-hearted Bucky had said.

The youth had begged to stay. Bucky had allowed him his wish. Now the youth would tremble and stare blankly at nothing no more. A Spanish bullet had plowed through his heart halfway up San Juan Hill.

Cal moved closer.

"Don't touch him, please," the undersheriff pleaded.

Cal stopped.

Sheriff Hawkins was slowly sinking downward. His bottom would miss his chair. The undersheriff scurried around the table.

He placed a chair directly under the sheriff's descending bottom. The sheriff landed on the chair. His head went forward and lay on his arms on the table. He apparently slept.

Cal glanced at the stairway. Mary Malone stood on the landing. She wore a blue dressing robe and held a heavy ceramic water-pitcher. Cal got the impression she'd been coming down for ice-water.

She said, "I'll call his mother." She disappeared upstairs. Soon she returned with Mickie whose big form was encased in a green dressing robe. Mickie laid a hand affectionately on Sheriff Hawkins' head.

"Did you see it, Cal?"

Cal nodded.

"Describe how he acted, please?"

Cal did.

Mickie listened carefully, tears in her eyes. When Cal had finished she said, "The attack is ended now. Just let him sleep for a while. He'll be all right when he awakens."

Cal said nothing. The undersheriff was silent. Mary Malone looked dark and small and lovely, her eyes on the sleeping Sheriff Hawkins.

Mickie kissed her boy on the forehead. "He'll be all right now," she said. Her voice was husky.

She returned upstairs.

Chapter Twelve

Heavy-set Mike Western rode two miles straight east to his homestead shack after the twin's giving him the beating. He met nobody because all were at the Graham farewell party.

He was glad he'd not run into anybody. He was ashamed of being beaten by the twins. Only the twins and two others—Mel Powers and Cal Sherman—had seen him beaten.

His collie came out to meet him. He pushed the dog—his only friend—to one side. He hurried to the horse-trough. There he washed his bloody face. The water was tepid, but it was water—and that was what counted.

His life was in danger. Well did he know that. Mel Powers had used him and Mel Powers had no more need for him. He felt sure that had not Cal Sherman been a witness the twins would have killed him on Powers' orders.

Common sense told him to go into hiding.

He'd skipped the country before. Two years ago down in Wyoming he'd long-looped cattle and run his trail-brand on them before driving them out to sell to butchers in the trail-towns.

The local ranchers had soon got wise. They'd been riding toward Western's cabin when he'd discovered this and saddled up and rode hell-bent-for-leather out of the country.

The ranchers had all packed catch-ropes, of course—but those ropes at that particular time did not pack hondos made of brass or merely tied into the rope. Instead of slip-hondos, the ropes had packed hangman nooses.

He was one of the original farmers having arrived a little over a year ago. Water dripping from his hair, he went into his cabin, where he hastily scrawled a note directed to his neighbor on the west, Sig Nelson.

Dear Sig: I have to leave for a few days. If I do not come back all I own is yours and Hilda's and your family's.

Signed: Michael Vernon Western.

P.S. Collie goes with me.

He had a few supplies in the house. A bachelor lived and ate simply, he ruefully thought, and tried to grin at the thought—but his swollen lips forbade such a luxury.

Anger beat in him toward Powers and his two gundogs. He forced it into the background. Anger had no place here. What he now required was logic—cold and constructive.

He was careful to overlook no cartridges for his .30-30 Winchester rifle or his Colt hang-gun. His supplies gathered, he went to his horse, tied his belongings behind the saddle, and swung up.

He reined in, checking last details. He had no stock tied in the barn. His two milk cows and work horses were on pasture. They had water in the ditch. His chickens—?

Sig would probably be over this evening unless he got too drunk at the Graham's. He'd feed the cluckers.

He rode to his east gate. Beyond his were no more homesteads. His was the last one-hundred-and-sixty to the east.

He opened and closed the gate without dismounting. He then rode northeast and dropped down into Mad Horse River buckbrush and timber. Once hidden from any eyes, he swung west, heading for high Signal Butte.

He'd rest there until his beating healed. Already one eye was swollen shut. He needed two good eyes for what he planned.

He did not know that ahead of him rode Mel Powers and the gun-hung twins, also heading for Signal Butte. Hadn't one of the kids down-town—the spies—reported he'd seen sign of somebody camping on the Butte for a few days?

Where the hell had that bastard Cal Sherman come from?

Mel Powers gave lanky Cal Sherman some thought. He did not fear the man. His thoughts held more curiosity than possible threat. Sherman was in Mad Horse town for some definite purpose.

Powers was sure of that. If Sherman didn't have a purpose in town, then why did he go around peering into abandoned buildings?

He had circle riders out all the time. None had reported seeing Cal Sherman ride into Mad Horse Basin. He knew Sherman had slipped past his outside men, for Sherman didn't have wings. Neither had his big buckskin horse. Both hadn't flown like eagles into the basin.

And that pretty gambler—Mary Malone. What was she doing in Mad Horse town? Mad Horse had no extra money. And a gambler—a good gambler—worked towns with money.

And the woman was a good gambler, he'd learned. Try her on poker, blackjack, any game you wanted—and she knew how to play it and play it well. He tested her across the green-topped table. And she'd won.

High on stirrups, the twins proper ahead and behind, the white-clad cowman looked about, and although there was little grass because of the short rain, he liked what he saw.

For all his eyes fell on, he claimed. His father had driven Texas longhorns into this region when it had been the buffalo-hunting ground of the savage Blackfoot and the blood-hungry Sioux.

His father's long-gun and short-arm had eliminated both the buffalo and the redskin who lived off him. For thirty years the word of a Powers in this wilderness had been the word of the king.

You did what a Powers told you or you got out. And if you didn't get out, you got killed.

But the day of the big cattleman—the man who ran thousands of head over Uncle Sam's land—was going and, in many places, already gone. Mel Powers was no fool. You either changed or you were like the Indian—you were eliminated. The redskin hadn't changed. White men's rifles had been needed to make him see the light.

He'd change. And profit in the change, he told himself.

He looked at his two black-suited gunmen. He knew they must have been sweltering under their black suits and black shirts. Black attracted heat; white repelled it.

He looked at the two identical faces. Each face was set with a grim doggedness. Each face portrayed a low mentality. He knew they were a step above a loony.

He corrected that to two steps, not one. They were so stupid and slow-thinking they had no place in their makeup for disloyal thoughts . . . or acts. They walk into any guns he ordered them to.

He'd met the two in South St. Paul when back on some cow-business. A cow-buyer there had been slow on paying. Powers had caught the Northern Pacific at Billings and gone to collect . . . and he'd met the twins.

They'd been hanging around a cowman-saloon, down on their luck and broke. Their eyes had glowed when he'd described the black suits and the two guns—or one, which sometimes they packed.

He'd probably given them lessons in how to draw, level and shoot. They'd learned fast. He'd learned from Max later that Max and Ted had pulled off a few jobs for the local gangsters in St. Paul.

"We could shoot good afore you learned us, boss," Max had said.

Now Max, proper paces ahead and to the right, turned on stirrups and asked, "You say Signal Butte, boss?"

"Signal Butte," Mel Powers clipped.

Max looked at Ted, right paces behind and to the left. "He said Signal Butte, Ted."

"Signal Butte," Ted said.

Max asked, "What're we goin' do on Signal?"

"Trap field mice."

Max spoke to Ted. "We're goin' trap mice."

Ted laughed. "He's a great boss. Funny as hell, he is. Ain't you now, Mr. Powers?"

"A real laugh-maker," Powers said.

"We sure whupped thet sonofabitch Newberger with our ropes," Ted said.

Max said, "Not Newberger. Mr. Snelson."

"Oh, Snelson, eh?" Ted said.

Mel Powers said not a word. He rode hard and high on oxbows, pushing his bronc, his gunmen matching his speed, maintaining distance correctly.

"You had us whup him 'cause he lied to you, eh?" Max spoke to Powers.

Powers nodded.

"He won't lie to you ag'in," Max assured.

Mel Powers again nodded. Liar, eh? Faint excuse for almost killing a man. But he'd had to think of some reason. And branding Western a liar had been the first to enter his mind.

Not a substantial excuse, by any means. Had Sherman swallowed it? Mel Powers had his doubts. Sherman was no moron in the class of Ted and Max. Sherman had a head on him, Powers guessed.

Then, Signal Butte loomed ahead.

Signal Butte rode in the center of a huge gravel-bedded alluvial moraine. Centuries before it had been a huge round flat topped mesa. Millions of years of water and snow and ice had worn it down. Now it sat on its high bed the king of all other buttes for miles and miles around.

Sagebrush and buckbrush grew on the flat. When the Butte began to lift, the sagebrush fell back; from base to high ceiling Signal Butte was covered by scraggly buckbrush, squat cedar, and tons of boulders, some as huge as houses, others ordinary in size.

Shod hoofs ground on gravel. You could ride halfway up the Butte. On its southern base was a spring. The spring now had little water. Drought had affected it, also.

The trio watered horses there. Somebody had scooped a small basin in the gravel. The water was shallow and the basin small but the water was clear and sweet.

"Lots of horse prints around here," Ted said.

Max searched the ground. "Turds are of all sizes and age," he said. He ground one with his boot. "About a week old, I'd say."

They could ride no further. Various trails ran upward. Some were made by cottontail rabbits and other wildings. Some towns-kids had made for it was a nice hike out from town and from the top of Signal Butte you could see for miles and miles.

You could pretend you were an Injun scouting for buffalo. Or a war-party of Crows, or Blackfeet, or even Assiniboines. You could be Sitting Bull or Crazy Horse or Gall.

"Go up the top," Mel Powers ordered. "Both of you. I wait here."

The twins didn't like that. Both hated manual labor, but nonetheless they went. They were drawing down a hundred bucks and food and bed a month. Where else could a guy get such a princely sum and just walk around—swagger around—with one gun on your hip sometimes, the next time a gun on each hip?

A hundred feet up, Max glanced back. Mel Powers was on the ground with his rifle under his arm looking up at them.

Max panted, "The sonofabitch."

"Why say that?" Ted asked.

"He's off his horse. Standin' there, with his rifle. Expect any minute to lose a boothell, an' hear the rifle report sing out."

"I doubt if he'll fire."

"Why do you say that?"

"He ain't jokin' an' kiddin' today. He's plumb serious. I wonder why he had us beat up on that damn' farmer?"

"I don't know. I enjoyed it. Did you?"

Ted grinned. "Now thet you mention it, brother, I was a bit happy about givin' thet bastard the maguey."

No bullet came from Mel Powers.

The twins continued climbing. Below them the grand valley spread out all directions. Mountains hemmed it in on all sides except the east where the badlands stretched lonesome and eroded toward Dakota.

Below, Mel Powers sat on a boulder in the shade of a chokecherry tree, carefully poised on the big rock's edge, a blue bandana between his seat and the sandstone to protect his white pants.

Sometimes he wished he'd selected black and made his gun-guards dress in white, for black soiled less easily. White was always getting dirty almost immediately.

But black was so damned hot in the summer. Of course, Montana had six months of winter when you seldom or ever saw the sun in the daytime and had more chance of seeing the Northern Lights at night. Black and white carried the same degree of heat—which was nil—in winter-time.

Things were adding up too slowly, he thought, taking his mind to the present. By this time he should have had at least thirty farmers moved in—and thirty was the outside number he'd determined.

Get thirty in, have them build dams each one, get their fields in alfalfa, get irrigation ditches in—well, thirty fields of even no more than eighty acres each, could sure feed a lot of head of hungry cattle come winter-time.

He stretched his legs. He admired the crease in his white trousers. He paid homage to his snow-white Hyer boots. His eyes lingered on his silver-white Crockett spurs, white even to star-rowels and white leather straps.

Suddenly, he thought of Mike Western.

Had not Cal Sherman been present, he'd have allowed his twins to whip the farmer to death. He'd given Mike Western orders to be hidden in the brush to watch Hersey, Snodgrass and Martin to jump the farmer, Si Graham.

The three dead men had been instructed to warn Graham, nothing more. Instead, not only Graham had been killed but also dead were his three men. What in the name of billy hell had happened out there in those foothills that savage morning?

Had Mike Western been there, scouting from the brush as ordered, he'd have seen what had taken place, and accordingly would have reported back. But he hadn't been there.

He'd been snoring in Mickie O'Hannigan's hotel . . . The shade was good. He'd pounded the saddle a lot lately. He dozed off. He was almost asleep when the twins returned.

"Nobody on top," Max said.

Ted said, "Horse-crap there. Looked about five or six days old."

"He didn't taste it," Max said. "If he had, he'd known to the hour how old it was."

"Shut your big mouth," Ted said.

"Other tracks?" Mel Powers asked.

"Boots. Big boots. Not kid boots. Tracks of town kids, of course—but a grown man has roosted there for some time. Not there now, though."

"You told me that," Mel Powers snapped. "Anythin' else? Find any pistol or rifle casin's?"

"Twenty-two empties," Ted informed.

"Town children," Powers said. "Layin' there with a little .22 Marlin or Winchester an' waitin' for cottontails to stick their heads out from under the boulders. Used to do it myself when I was a kid."

"Hard to think of you as a boy," Max said.

Mel Powers gave the man a hard look. He then realized there was no insult meant. The man just spoke what had first come to his mind. He meant nothing sinister. Nor was he joking. He as just merely talking.

Powers did not answer. He was in deep thought.

One point stood out. The twins had seen a man's bootprints on Signal Butte's crest. That alone meant two points.

Point one was that no man had any reason to climb the high hill, especially in the present heat wave. Nothing on top of Signal Butte held any attraction for a grown man.

The man had climbed the butte for only one reason, Mel Powers deducted. That was to gain a high altitude to be able to carefully look over the entire basin below.

The other point was that the man had worn high-heeled riding boots. That meant he'd been a man on horseback. He'd apparently kept his horse hidden in the high brush surrounding the spring. This accounted for the accumulation of horse turds.

This substantiated his theory that a man had deliberately climbed Signal Butte after hiding his horse and from the top of the butte had carefully and for a couple of days watched the doings and goings on in Mad Horse Basin, stretching miles all directions below.

Who had that man been?

Mel Powers could think of only one candidate and that was Cal Sherman, the only new arrival in Mad Horse for many days. Still, the theory that Sherman hid out for days on the butte before riding into town didn't hold water, for Sherman had no reason for hiding out—or had he?

Mel Powers abandoned such thinking. He gave his attention to his cattle as he and his gunmen rode east in the direction of Mad Horse town.

His cows were thin. Grass was scarce. They came to Wisdom Creek, a branch of the Mad Horse. The creek had stopped flowing. He could never remember a time when it hadn't been flowing.

But now it was mere potholes. These were green with scum. Mosquitoes rose by the thousands.

The banks of the potholes were slimy mud. The cattle had to wade out through treacherous blue mud to reach the water. One had two cows bogged down. They'd sunk to their bellies in the mud while trying to wade out to the precious dirty water.

"Remember these cows," he told the twins.

Both of the twins nodded simultaneously. Neither spoke. Both knew it was not their job to pull the cows out of the bog. They were hired to ride gun, not dirty their fine black clothing with blue mud.

Mel Powers did not know that two miles west of town a man and his saddle-horse were hidden a mere hundred feet away in the high buckbrush surrounding the south bank of Wisdom Creek.

The man's dog lay beside him as the hidden man knelt, Winchester rifle in hand, the .30-30 pointed the general direction of Mel Powers and his twin gun-guards. The collie was well-trained.

He neither whined or made any noise. The man recognized the dim forms of Powers and the twins, but he could not see them clearly because both of his eyes were swollen almost shut.

His face was marked forever. His face bore open wounds that would in time scab over and after the scabs fell off would show terrible scars.

This man wanted to kill Mel Powers. He wanted to kill the twins, too. He knew it would be three to one odds if he could center the rifle on Powers and pull the trigger. And kill the cowman. . . .

He'd then kill the twins, one at a time . . . unless one of the trio killed him, first.

But he couldn't see the trio clearly. Each and his horse were no more than drifting shadows in the gathering dusk. Finally he slowly lowered his rifle, the trio riding past and soon out of sound.

He put his hand on the dog's head. The dog twisted his head around so he could lick the man's hand. The man then put both arms around the dog's neck. He wept great tears into the shaggy coat.

The smell of the dog's hair was in his nostrils. The feel of the long hair was rough on his face. He then put the area back of his right ear against the dog. Now the thick fur didn't hurt his face.

He said, "I'm goin' kill that sonofabitch. . . .

He spoke softly.

"An' I'll kill them damn' twins, too, the sonsofbitches!"

Here his voice hardened slightly.

He told the dog, "We wait here until the night comes an' then moon. . . ."

He had a sudden plan. He realized he only needed the supplies and cartridges in the Bemis grain sack tied behind his saddle. He did not need his horse. He then out of nowhere became owner of another plan.

This he consumated by trapping a cottontail rabbit with a horse-hair snare. He set the trap—made out of tail-hairs on his horse—in a rabbit runway he could scarcely see.

The collie told him when the snare had a young cottontail. The collie shook the cottontail dead. The man took the cottontail from the collie's jaws.

He then did a strange thing.

He took out his pocket-knife. He opened the longest blade. And then he cut the rabbit's throat.

Blood came from the throat. He then cut the head off. More blood came. He held the rabbit over his saddle. He felt to make sure the blood had got on the fork, the cantle, the seat.

He then pulled the hide from the rabbit and tossed it to the dog who caught it in midair and began eating the flesh.

The man tied the horse's bridle-reins in a knot so they'd not drop and make the horse step on one and so ground-tie himself. He then hit the horse on the rump with his hand and the horse galloped away and then became lost in the distance, both in sound and sight.

Four hours later, the man and the collie were on the summit of Signal Butte. The man had four canteens of water he'd taken from the spring. The night air was blistering hot.

"As hot at midnight as it was at noon," the man told the dog. "And two weeks from now, there might be a blizzard. Montana weather, eh?"

The man lay down. He went to sleep. He'd stay until

he could see again. Then he'd head out with his rifle to kill three men.

Soon he snored.

He dreamed of his homestead. His neighbor was a Norwegian named Sig Nelson. He'd given his homestead to Sig, hadn't he? Or had he, really?

He did not know that at that moment Sig Nelson had just ridden his old plow-horse Nancy into the homestead's yard. "Where is your lamp, Mike?" the Norwegian had asked in his broken English.

Nelson had, of course, received no answer. Nelson frowned in his slow, deliberate way. Maybe Mike had gone to town to the saloon? But where was his collie? He never took the collie to town with him.

Again, he called. Again, no reply. He dismounted. He stood in front of the open door.

Something was wrong. The door should have been closed. Mike always kept it closed against mosquitos because he had no screen-door.

Frowning, Nelson entered.

That afternoon Mike and the twins and Mel Powers had ridden to the south end of the Graham homestead to where Cal Sherman had been looking around. Mike had not returned.

Why had he gone there with Powers?

Sig Nelson didn't know. Olaf Hanson had told him that Powers and his twins had ridden in and Powers had said, "Come along with us, Western," and Mike had gone with them.

He'd looked for Mike to come back and finish their horseshoe game but Mike hadn't.

Hanson had told him Mike had ridden out of the Graham's lower east gate, apparently heading for his homestead shack.

Why hadn't he ridden back to finish their horseshoe throwing?

Another thing didn't make sense. Mike liked his booze. He'd just been getting drunk when he'd ridden off with Powers. By all rights Mike should have returned and finished the drunk he was starting on.

Sig Nelson dug in a shirt pocket. His matches were there along with his eatin'-tobaccer. He finally got two matches segregated. He lit one. He saw the kerosene lamp on the table.

He slipped the chimney from the prongs, aiming to light the lamp. The chimney fell from his fingers. It hit the floor and made a scattering sound as it broke into many pieces.

Sig Nelson told Sig Nelson, "You're purty drunk, Sig."

Hilda would have another lamp chimney. Hilda was a good woman. She figured ahead for him and the whole family. God bless you, Hilda!

He touched the match to the wick. Without a chimney the light was yellow and weak but still strong enough to show Western's note.

Sig Nelson picked it up. He held it close to the flame. He'd gone to only the third year of school in Tromso. He had trouble reading Norwegian and more trouble reading English.

His lips moved. He deciphered words. He then put down the note and scratched his head. This didn't make sense.

Something was wrong here. . . .

Chapter Thirteen

Two mornings later Cal talked to Bea Graham right after she'd reported for work in the Mercantile. "Your brother and your mother? They get off?"

"Yesterday morning, Cal. The others sure gave them a send-off. Ray Jernigan and Matt Smith even rode with them to where the road turns south and goes through the hills toward Billings."

"About twenty odd miles."

Bea glanced at him. "You know that road. Did you ride in from the south—from the direction of Billings?"

Cal's tongue had slipped. "I was over that road a few years back. Nope, I rode in from the north—from the direction of Lewistown."

Bea nodded.

"What are you going to do with your farm?"

"I really don't know. I can't handle it and work here at the same time. And if I hired somebody to farm it—Well, it would take my wages here to pay his and what would I eat on?" She laughed.

Cal pointed out she had some hay stacks. "Maybe Mel Powers would buy them?"

"I asked him. He gave no definite answer. He said he'd think it over and winter was a long, long way off."

"Do you want to sell your homestead entry?"

"Mama said to sell it. She was offered four hundred dollars—from Matt Smith—but she's holding out for more money. She'd like at least five hundred, she told me before leaving."

Cal nodded.

Tears came to Bea's eyes. "I already miss Mama and Bill. Oh, dreadfully, Cal."

Cal had no words. He was doing arithmetic. He still had his mustering-out pay of three hundred and eighty dollars. Three hundred and eighty from five hundred made one hundred and twenty. He had eighty bucks in cash. That meant he was forty bucks shy of five hundred.

Mickie owed him a few day's pay but far from forty dollars. He might be able to borrow the forty from her.

He considered other angles. His room and board cost him nothing, as long as he tended bar for Mickie. He had forenoons and much of the day to work on the homestead.

Of course, he still owned his homestead rights. He could file on a homestead himself. He then remembered the alfalfa field and the dam and the water behind the dam.

Si Graham and his son had done a lot of work on the homestead. The house, of course, wasn't much count, nor was the brush-barn—but all in all, five hundred seemed a fair price.

"I'll need to borrow a few dollars," Cal said.

Bea thoughtfully said, "I have to be honest, Cal. Mr. Powers asked me to hold the sale back until he and I had a talk."

Always some fly in the ointment. . . . "When will that be?"

"He didn't set a date."

Cal said, "Then you haven't much to go on. He can keep you on pins and needles for a long time if you pay attention to him."

Bea hesitated, said, "Frankly, I'm afraid of him."

Cal didn't ask why the fear. He remembered Mike Western's lash-cut face, the blood. "I understand. But let's do it this way, eh?"

Bea looked at him. "What way, Cal?"

"I got mornings free. I'll ride out and take care of things and work around—for free—until my shift comes at the saloon. Wait a minute, please—there's another catch."

"What's that?"

"If you're spending nights on your homestead, I can't spend the rest of the night after shift there. Man alive, wouldn't this town buzz if I did!"

"Mrs. Halverson said she'd spend nights with me but I'd rather stay in town. The Russells have offered me board and room here at their home."

The Russells ran the Mercantile. Cal had heard that Mr. Russell had worked long for Mel Powers' father and after his father's death Powers had rented the store out to Russell.

"You'll stay in town, then?"

"Okay. And you'll spend nights after you get off work at the homestead?"

Cal nodded. "Be a nice ride in the moonlight for me. Anybody seen or heard anything about Mike Western?"

"Not a word, Cal. The other farmers—they're worried, too. If we told them what we know—that the twins beat Western—I wouldn't be surprised to see the farmers ride into town and challenge Powers."

"They're that hot under the collar?"

"They're not so much angry as they are afraid. Graham got killed, Mike Western disappeared—well, you understand."

Cal seriously nodded. "We'd best keep our secret, like you say. I'll talk to Mary and put her wise."

"We three could be in danger," Bea slowly said.

Cal had thought of that, also. He and the two women—and Mike Western—Mel Powers might try to silence them so nobody would ever know of the beating the twins had given Western—

Then common-sense came in. Mel Powers was powerful on this drought-stricken Montana range but not powerful enough to kill three people to keep their mouths shut.

Especially when two of the three were women, Cal reasoned. A man harm a woman on this grass and that man would be in serious trouble.

"I doubt that, Bea."

"What makes you say that?"

Cal explained. Bea had just come from the east. There were lots of women there. Here on the Montana frontier women were scarce. He pointed out that even a woman as huge and unattractive as Mickie had had many proposals of marriage, he'd been told.

Bea laughed. "You've made me feel better," she said. "We'll just leave it all in Western's hands."

"Wherever Western is," Cal said. "He might be dead, somewhere along the road, you know. He was beat up pretty awful."

Bea shuddered.

A customer came in to buy a handful of shingle nails so Cal left. He was in front of the barber-shop when a small boy said, "Mr. Powers an' the twins were out on Signal Butte day afore yesterday, Mr. Sherman."

Cal stopped. "Signal Butte? Where's that?"

The boy pointed northwest. You could just see the south slope of the Butte between the two buildings. "That's Signal Butte."

Cal scowled. "You mean they went to the top of that high hill?"

"Not Mr. Powers. The twins did."

"How'd you know all this?"

"Pinky an' me was up on the butte huntin' cottontails with our .22s. We heard the twins comin' so we hid back in the rocks an' watched."

"What'd they do up there?"

"They seemed to be lookin' for tracks. Pinkie an' me saw a man's tracks up there. Cowboy boots, the heels showed us—an' what would a man be doin' on Signal?"

"You got me," Cal said.

"Horse turds up there, too," the boy said.

"Why are you telling me this?" Cal asked.

"I need a nickle."

Cal rubbed his jaw. "I don't understand, Jimmy. Why didn't you just come right out and ask me to lend you five cents?"

"Well, I wanted to be of some service, first. I'm no beggar an' I—Well, that's the story."

Cal dug into his pocket. "I said *lend,* not *give.* Remember that. Your father told me at the bar last night that you make twenty-five cents a week milking your cows."

"He tol' you thet?"

"He did. And you get paid each Sundy morning. So next Sunday I except you to pay me back, savvy?"

"My ol' man talks too much. Sunday mornin', Mr. Sherman."

Cal continued on toward the saloon, thinking over what the boy had said. Had Jimmy been warning him? That was impossible. Nobody had seen him and Smoky on top of Signal Butte.

He put points together. The twins had scaled the Butte. They'd evidently been working on Powers' orders. Nobody but an idiot—or a kid hunting cottontails—would climb the Butte in this heat.

Cal dismissed his forebodings. Possibly Mel Powers suspected he'd been hiding on the Butte, and possibly he'd not. Still, why had he sent the twins up, in such a torrid sun?

Harsh words broke his train of thought. "You still stickin' aroun', drifter?"

Cal stopped. He was in front of Half Circle V's office. The words had come from Mel Powers who sat behind his desk close to the open window.

"Drifter?" Cal asked, anger forming.

"I said *drifter,* remember?"

The word *drifter* was an insult. A drifter never worked, bummed grub, had no self respect. You might just as well call a man a sonofabitch.

No, the word *sonofabitch* was an insult to your mother. That made her a bitch dog. Drifter was a personal insult, a reflection upon a man's manhood.

It was one of Montana's fighting words. When you called a man a drifter you had to be prepared for a fight—either with fists or guns. Unless, of course, the man was an abject coward.

Cal said slowly, "You talk big, Powers. But would

you have such a big mouth if those two black-dressed guns were not behind you?"

Mel Powers did not answer Cal's question. "I haven't cottoned to you, Sherman, since the day I first laid eyes on you, in the school house."

"Maybe the feeling is mutual?"

Powers pulled air deep into his lungs. "I'll look for you to leave town inside of a few days, Sherman."

"That an order?"

"Read it as you see fit."

Cal laughed shortly. "You set no time limit, Powers."

"None is needed."

Cal looked at Mel Powers and Powers looked at Cal Sherman. Cal then remembered the twins climbing Signal Butte. He was pretty sure that Powers suspected him of making the boot-tracks on Signal. And that the horse droppings had come from under the tail of no horse other than Smoky.

Sheriff Ike Monday had waddled in. Cal had caught a side-glance of the obese sheriff.

"Please, no trouble, men," Monday said.

Cal said, "He challenged me, sheriff. I was just walking by minding my own business."

"Look across the street," Powers said.

Sheriff Hank Hawkins and his undersheriff had left the pool hall and were crossing the street, hands on their holsters. Cal glanced back at Powers. Powers watched the pseudo sheriff and his assistant coming his direction.

Cal had never before seen such hate glistening in a human's eyes. Powers seemed to be possessed by anger. His very lips shook. His hand on the desk trembled.

"Let him come," Powers told Sheriff Monday. "I'll

have to kill him, sooner or later—and it might jus' as well be now."

Cal looked at the twins. They'd come afoot and had moved in behind their boss. Cal noticed each packed two guns, each .45 tied down. This evidently was their day to buckle on double-strength hardware.

"You won't kill him when he packs an unloaded gun," Sheriff Ike Monday gritted. "You do, an' this burg'll be dynamited apart, Powers."

"I own the goddamned town," Powers snarled, "an' a man can blow up his own property, cain't he?"

Monday said, "You'd not be alive to see the town go up, Powers. You'd be danglin' from the end of a rope down on Hangman's Tree down street, an' you know it. Mel, for God's sake, use your head!"

A boy standing close by said, "Jimmy ran for Mickie, Sheriff."

Cal looked upstreet. Mickie and Mary Malone came running out of the saloon. They hurried down the steps. Mickie stumbled slightly on the worn plank sidewalk, but Mary caught her and the saloon-keeper had her balance again.

Cal looked at Sheriff Hawkins and his deputy. The women would not reach the pair in time. Cal moved forward. He met Sheriff Hawkins on the edge of the planks.

He grabbed the youth. Hawkins fought him, cursing him. He was wiry and young and stronger than Cal had expected. Sheriff Monday wrestled with the undersheriff. Finally, Cal got both arms around Hawkins from the rear, and held the struggling youth, with Hawkins' head down as he tried to bite Cal's hands.

"Hold him for me, Cal!" Mickie screamed.

Mary arrived first. She said, "Sheriff, be a good

boy!" and Sheriff Hawkins spat at her. Mary jumped to one side, the sputumn missed, and she looked at Cal, pleading in her dark eyes.

"Hold him, Cal," she said.

Cal nodded. He glanced at the real sheriff. Monday had his hands full with the pseudo undersheriff. Monday panted hard, trying to hold.

Cal glanced at Powers' office. Powers now stood on the sidewalk, watching. He seemed amused. He smiled tightly. Behind him stood Ted, proper paces to the left, standing in the street dust.

Max stood behind, also proper.

Mickie then reached her son. She said, "I'll take over, Cal," and she put both her arms around Sheriff Hawkins.

Hawkins stopped struggling. He put his arms around Mickie. He said, "Mama, I love you."

The undersheriff had stopped struggling. Cal saw Sheriff Ike Monday stagger to the planks. Monday sat down and put his head between his hands and caught Montana air in huge gulps.

"I love you, too, my son."

Sheriff Hawkins looked over his mother at Mel Powers and the black-garbed gunmen.

Sheriff Hawkins said, "Do I have to kill you, Powers?"

Mel Powers smiled. "Do I have to kill you, Hawkins?"

Hawkins said, "You've cheapened me—and my office and star—before the entire town. You've shot my boots almost under me and in public view."

"And that'll happen again unless you tell me where you got that double eagle," Powers said shortly.

Cal had expected Sheriff Hawkins to go into one of

his spasms at the mention of a bullet-dance, but the make-believe sheriff didn't.

Hawkins said, "You stop citizens on the street. You hollered from out your window. You insulted Mr. Sherman. The constitution of the United States gives each and every citizen his privacy."

"Hear, hear," Max said.

People had gathered about. Cal noticed a few farmers in the group. Sheriff Hawkins opened his mouth again but Mickie clamped her hand over his mouth. He did not struggle. He now was calm. He gently pushed his mother's hand aside.

He said, "You want me to speak no more, mama?"

"No more, son." Mickie spoke to Cal. "Help me get him to his bed upstairs, Cal."

"Certainly."

Mickie and Cal went upstreet, Sheriff Hawkins between them. The sheriff's head lolled. He walked unsteadily. His undersheriff trailed behind. Cal looked back at Sheriff Ike Monday.

A short man bent over Monday. Cal recognized him as the town doctor. Even as Cal watched, the doctor got Monday to his feet and, with the aid of another man, started him toward the doctor's office, two doors down street from Powers' headquarters.

Sheriff Hawkins was limp and almost unconscious when Mickie and Mary and Cal got his clothing from him and put him to bed. Mickie wept softly. Mary was solemn and thoughtful.

"Maybe I should send him to Warm Springs," Mickie said chokingly.

Mary was silent. Cal had no words.

Mickie said, "I'd leave with him. I'd have to be close to him." She sat on a chair Mary had put in place. "I couldn't live without seeing him."

Cal looked at Mary Malone. Her dark eyes held tears. He designated toward the door with his head.

He and Mary left.

Mary caught his arm. "Thanks, Cal."

"For what?"

"For having an arm I can catch onto to." They walked in silence halfway down the hall. "I guess a girl never gets to the point where she doesn't miss her father."

"Or a man his mother."

They went down the stairs together. He caught her faint perfume and liked its sweetness.

The saloon was without customers. All still stood in front of Powers' office and the doctor's office.

Powers and his guns had left the street. Cal judged they'd gone back into Half Circle V's office.

Jimmy came running, knifing through the crowd. He dashed into the saloon. "He's—he's dead," he said hurriedly.

"Who's dead?" Cal asked.

"Sheriff Monday!"

Cal looked at Mary. Mary's face was pale. Cal remembered hearing that the sheriff had had previous heart attacks. Evidently wrestling with the under-sheriff—coupled with the heat—had been too much for the lawman's heart.

Mary said, "Things are tightening up."

Cal Sherman could only nod.

Chapter Fourteen

Ten minutes after Sheriff Monday's death the county commissioners met in the courthouse on the end of the street. Chief Commissioner Mel Powers called the meeting to order.

The commissioners' job was to appoint a new sheriff. The body consisted of five men not counting Mel Powers. The five were all town residents who owed their bread and butter—and the clothes on their backs—to Powers' Half Circle V spread.

"Mel's always wanted to be sheriff," Mickie told Mary and Cal, "an' now's the bastard's time!"

Powers was unamimously elected sheriff. All five others voted for him. "Some won't want to," Mickie added, "but they'll vote for him, anyway. You don't vote against the gink who puts grub in your mouth an' the mouths of your family. You'd like to, in some case—but you don't dare."

The twins were voted in as deputies.

"A town without law," Mickie said.

Sheriff Hank Hawkins was upstairs sleeping, his undersheriff sitting beide Hawkins' bed. Hawkins' deputies were seated on the floor, quietly talking about the sudden turn of events.

Soon Mel Powers and his deputies patroled the streets—all two of them. Townspeople watched but were silent. Cal Sherman detected a tightness around this town, a band of hate and despair. Or was he imagining things?

Mary Malone was gone the next morning.

Apparently she left after midnight. Cal and she had closed the bar and card tables at midnight and Cal had said goodnight to her as she opened her room's door.

Next morning, she was gone—and her bed apparently unslept in, for it was made-up.

Mickie discovered Mary's disappearance. The women had breakfast together at eleven in Mickie's room. Mary didn't show up. Mickie walked down-hall and found Mary's room empty.

She pounded on Cal's door but Cal had got out of his sougans at six and had ridden to the Graham ranch to do the chores, Smoky spooky and with high hoofs, rested and wanting a long, hard trail.

Mickie and Sheriff Hawkins drove out to the Graham farm behind Mickie's matched chestnut geldings in a bright red spring-wagon with a black cowhide cover against the glaring Montana sun. Sheriff Hawkins' deputies trailing on horseback.

Cal had finished slopping the hogs and feeding the dog and chickens and was seated in the shade of the brush-barn rubbing Neatsfoot oil into a harness's tugs.

"Mary's gone," Mickie said.

"What do you mean by that?" Cal asked.

The deputies dismounted and Sheriff Hank Hawkins leaped to the ground, then turned and courteously helped his adopted mother, with Mickie explaining to Cal as she left the spring-wagon.

"Where's her buckskin?" Cal asked.

The buckskin and Mary's saddle and riding gear were also gone from the town stable, Mickie stated. "An' her bed hadn't been slept in. I had my Sioux girl change linen on her bed yesterday. The linen hadn't been slept on. I opened the bed to make sure."

"She must have left right after I said goodnight to her," Cal observed. "You say her personal belongings—clothes, things like that—are still in her room?"

"They are."

"Then she must intend to come back." Suddenly it dawned on Cal why Mickie was taking this departure so serious. "My God, Mickie! You don't suppose somebody's taken her—by force—?"

"I've thought that over very seriously on the way out from town," the saloon-keeper said, "but I don't think she was kidnapped. First, she'd have fought like all billy-get-out and made some noise—"

"She have to be taken past your bedroom, too. And I suppose you had your door open, as usual."

"I did. But maybe I sleep sounder than I figure for she must have gone past my door."

"No note?"

"Nothing behind," Mickie said. She looked about. "This spread has got the makin's of a nice farm. I undertand it's for sale."

"Five hundred dollars takes over the homestead entry," Cal informed. "Bea told me. I lack less than a hundred."

"Six hundred now," Mickie corrected. "Rumor

around town that Mel Powers upped your ante a hundred."

Cal winced. "Well, farewell, dreams," he said.

Mickie said nothing. Sheriff Hank Hawkins said, "I feel like workin'. You got a ditch or two you need cleaned out, Mr. Sherman?"

"I sure have," Cal said. "There are three shovels here. We need two more. Sig Nelson'll have them."

"I'll ride over to his farm," the undersheriff said.

The sheriff's posse went to work, Sheriff Hawkins issuing orders. Mickie and Cal sat in the shade drinking cold lemonade Mickie had taken out from town, ice chunks still floating.

Mickie said no more about the purchase of this farm and Cal didn't bring up the subject, thinking that if he got his business running down-town he'd be plenty busy—maybe too busy to operate a farm and the business simultaneously.

Mickie quietly said, "With Powers as sheriff—with all the power that badge has—maybe I'd best get my son out of here. Would you consider leasin' my saloon for say a year?"

Cal hesitated. He wasn't in love with bartending . . . or running a saloon. He stalled with, "Give me a few days to think it over, please?"

"I'll approach Mary, too—that is, if she returns." Mickie poured lemonade. "Meanwhile, I'll keep my boy close to me an' out of harm's way, if I possibly can."

"How's your sheriff taking the new sheriff idea?"

"He's boilin' mad. So are his undersheriff and deputies. They all figure they should have been appointed the complete law agency, not Powers and those damn' twins."

"Always a problem. . . ."

"Always, Cal, always."

Sheriff Hawkins and his men did quite a bit of work straightening a side ditch choked with weeds. Afterward the whole law-force doused each other with water and profanity as they bathed naked in the long wooden water-tank. They were still whooping up a water-fight when Cal swung up on Smoky and neckreined him in the direction of town.

Mickie had told him she'd got One Step to take command and now it would soon be time for Cal to take over from One Step.

Farmer Louis Newbarger was repairing his north fence. Cal stopped to talk for a moment. "Reckon you done lost your purty little dark-haired girl friend, Mr. Sherman."

"You mean Miss Malone?"

"Yeah, Miss Malone. Last night some of my workhorses got out. I got up at three to look them up. Jes' gettin' light. An' I saw her—Miss Malone—off to the north, on the wagon road leadin' south to Billings."

"You sure it was her?"

"Danged sure, Mr. Sherman. I got me a pair of them army field-glasses last time in Billings—from the war, you know. They're right powerful. I saw her face clear 'cause daylight was gettin' strong. Not many hours of night here in Montany in the summertime."

Well, Cal thought, *at least we know which direction she went, if that means anything. . . .*

Cal changed the subject with, "Anybody seen hide or hair of Mr. Western?"

Nobody had. Western had apparently just fallen off the face of the earth. Why he left so suddenly—and where he went—were riddles being discussed by each and every farmer.

"How are your people taking it?" Cal asked.

Newbarger said the colony was worried and afraid at the same time. "Yeah, an' on edge, an' bad on edge, Mr. Sherman. Here was Si Graham—good, honest man—murdered. An' three dead Powers' han' layin' aroun' with Si. Hell, thet didn't make sense, an' mebbeso never will."

"It is a mystery," Cal conceded.

"Then for no apparent reason at all, Mike pulls out—dog an' all. Nobody knows which direction he went, and for why."

"What about the new sheriff department?"

"That's got us worried, too. Too much power in the hands of one man, even if his name is Powers. But the only thing us farmers can do is set back and watch an' keep our months shut—but, damn my buttons, these people seem about ready to bust their buttons—if the right button-buster came along."

"Things are a little tense."

"Now where in the billy-blue hell could Western be?"

Neither knew that Western was hiding on the crest of Signal Butte and for one day—the day after arrival—he'd been stone-blind, his eyes swollen completely closed.

He'd awakened from his dream-troubled sleep with both eyes matted shut. He saw nothing but darkness. Fear overcame him. He thought first he was blind and would stumble in darkness the rest of his life.

He clawed at his swollen eyes. He saw only the same blackness. He became desperate. He fairly ripped his right eye open. A faint crack of light penetrated. His fears ceased. He could see. His eyes were only swollen shut.

"I'll kill that Powers sonofabitch," he promised for the twentieth time.

Next morning he could see fairly well. Some boys came to the top of Signal Butte with their .22 rifles to still-hunt cottontails but he escaped discovery by lying quietly back in the brush and rocks. Finally the boys left. They had shot six cottontail rabbits.

They each broiled a rabbit over a fire, holding the flesh on long sticks. They left two skinned rabbits behind. Collie ate one; Western cooked the other. He slept better that night.

He lost track of days. Then the day came when he saw well and would see no better so that forenoon he ascended Signal Butte and with Collie he began the hike into Mad Horse town.

He walked to kill Mel Powers.

He did not know that the night before his horse had wondered into Sig Nelson's yard, saddle caked with dried blood. Sig immediately called his neighbors to a meeting at his farm. the horse and saddle being the center of discussion.

"He's been murdered," Louis Newbarger said. "That's his blood on the saddle. But where could his body be?"

Nobody had any idea where the dead man had fallen. "Montana hasn't no buzzards," Pancho Rios said. "Without buzzards, you can't tell where a dead thing is. Buzzards down in my old home used to tell us where a cow or something dead—even a dead man—was located."

Pancho Rios and his fat Maria and their eleven children had lived in the Territory of New Mexico before trekking north.

"When morning comes mebbeso we can trail back an' find where the horse came from," one farmer said.

Early next morning at daybreak they were busy trying to read tracks but they got nowhere. "None of us have

Apache blood in us,' Pancho said.

The truth of the matter that the horse had snagged a loop in his hanging bridle reins back in the Mad Horse River brush and had tied himself immobile for a few days.

A passing Half Circle V bull going down to a waterhole had hooked at the horse. The horse had leaped out of horn-range. In so doing he'd freed himself. He then taken a drink from the mud hole and grazed his way toward home, as horses do.

"We had better notify the sheriff," a farmer said.

One farmer laughed. "An' the new sheriff is nobody but Mr. Powers! I am beginning to believe like Si Graham! I now believe that when the time is right—and our homesteads are developed and in hay fields—and when all our work has been finished—"

"Hush, Papa, hush, please. You will have Mr. Powers on you, as he was on Mr. Graham—"

"I can say what I want, Mama."

Other farmers chipped in. More than one was getting suspicious of Mel Powers and his high-falutin' talk. They decided to go into town in a body and to carry arms.

The women, seeing their words were wasted, stated they would go along, as did the older children, so at high noon they drove in a group north to Mad Horse town, armed with rifles and shotguns and pistols—and hoping never would they have to use same.

Louis Newbarger led Mike Western's horse behind his lumber-wagon, the horse still carrying the blood stained saddle.

Louis Newbarger said to Sarah Newbarger, "Do not worry, wife. Everything will turn out all right."

Sarah had no reply. She stared ahead sightlessly into

the sullen heat. Sagebrush danced in the gray distance. Far ahead a mirage lingered, looking exactly like a lake where no lake was.

"Miss Malone came back last night," Louis said.

"How do you know? You haven't been in town for over a week."

"Isaac told me. He was in last night playin' a little cards. For once he won a few dollars."

"Good for him."

Louis Newbarger opened his mouth to say something else, looked at his wife's set profile, and then shut his mouth. He focused his attention on a horsefly sitting on his off-horse's rump.

The fly was intelligent. He'd selected a spot where the horse's tail could not hit him. Louis wondered if his buggy whip could hit the horse-fly. He decided to try.

The whiplash shot out. He missed the fly by a foot. The whip hit the horse who only swished his tail but went not a bit faster.

Not my day, the farmer ruefuelly thought. He thought of Mary Malone. Mary was about the prettiest woman he'd ever seen. He wondered where she'd been the last few days.

Mary had told Mickie and Cal she'd been to Harlington to the railroad station where she'd wired Washington, D.C., that perhaps it would be best that Fort Stanton—some sixty miles northwest—would send a few soldiers into Mad Horse Basin, seeing Sheriff Ike Monday had died and there had been four men killed around Mad Horse town in the last ten days.

"How come you have that authority?" Cal Sherman had asked.

Mary Malone explained that she was a government agent working for the Homestead Section out of

Washington. "My job is to see that the farmers get a fair shake. Uncle Sam put them on homesteads. Uncle Sam finally realized that they need protection at times, like down in Wyoming a few years ago when the cowmen shipped in a trainload of gunmen to drive out the farmers."

Cal nodded. Before the gunmen could swing into action, Uncle Sam had had his cavalry over in the farming area.

The gunmen had stopped, considered, then retreated for good.

"Well, that explains that," Mickie said. "I never at any time suspected, although it did seem strange a wanderin' woman gambler should come in."

"My father was a professional gambler. When just a little girl I traveled the world with him. I can't remember my mother. I still don't know if she died when I was a girl or if she and my father even took the trouble to get married, but that makes little difference. I'm here and I'm what I am."

"Well said," Cal said.

"What'd Washington say?" Mickie asked.

Mary showed the telegram. *Taking under consideration your suggestion*. Mickie handed it Cal to read. Cal handed it back with, "A very vague and uncertain reply."

He was glad Mary was back. He'd been worried about her, but he didn't tell her that.

"I look for federal troops to move in," Mary said. "Not many, but a few—and they'll supervise an election, a free one, for sheriff this time, I suppose."

"You'll not suffer from over popularity," Mickie assured.

Mary smiled. "That'll be nothing new. How is the

new sheriff getting along?"

"Throwing his weight around," Cal said.

Mary looked inquiringly at Mickie. "Still wants my bar and hotel," Mickie said. "Threatens to close me if I once more serve a drink—alcohol, of course—to a minor."

"I haven't been here long, but I've not seen you serve anybody that sure didn't look twenty-one, or over."

"He's referin' to my boy and his crowd. Powers claims I've served them hard liquor. I damn' near stuck his long nose in the jar holdin' the harmless mixture of lemonade and juices the boys call their liquor, but controled myself in time."

"What are you going to do?" Mary asked.

"Keep the boys out of the bar," Mickie said. "They can drink their harmless ade upstairs. I got to keep my boy out of Powers' way. Powers still is ravin' about thet twenty-buck gold piece."

Mary's face was solemn. It was more solemn next morning at eleven sharp. For three things happened at that hour, all occurring at the same clock-stroke by pure coincidence.

These three events blew Mad Horse town apart. . . .

Chapter Fifteen

First, Sheriff Hawkins escaped.

He'd been lying on the bed. His undersheriff and deputies sat on the floor playing poker. Suddenly their superior sat up. "I've made up my mind. I'm goin' kill Mel Powers!"

"How are you goin' get outa here?" the undersheriff asked.

Sheriff Hawkins leaped to his feet. "Like this!" He tore the sheets from his bed. He tied them together on one end. "We'll only need one or two more. Buck, get a couple from the linen-closet!"

"Where's it at?"

"In the hall, you idiot."

"I know where it's at," the undersheriff said. "I'll get them."

Again, two more knots. Then, the bed pulled next to the window, the top sheet tied to its near pillar. Sheriff Hawkins, as befitting his station, slid down first, undersheriff and deputies following. When on the ground one deputy pulled the undersheriff to one side, Sheriff Hawkins not noticing. "He's means business, don't he?"

The undersheriff wore a deep frown. "I think so. An' for one, I don't like it, an' not one bit."

"Me, neither."

Mickie and One Step were at the saloon's north side working in their vegetable garden which they irrigated by pumping water from Mad Horse River. Therefore the sheriff and his lagging undersheriff and deputies circled the building's south end and came out on Main Street.

Sheriff Hawkins called a halt. He wore only one gun, that on his right hip. "My plan in this. We walk past Powers' office—an', of course, he'll come out—I challenge him. I kill him. You boys take care of those two bastards in black, savvy?"

His law force nodded. He looked down street. His undersheriff and deputies looked worried. Knowing looks passed between them. They deserted the sheriff without his hearing them dart into the space between Powers' office and another building.

Without knowing it, Sheriff Hank Hawkins walked alone.

Twenty feet from Mel Powers' office, Ted stepped out on the planks, followed by Mel Powers with Max trailing the proper distance behind.

The three halted, blocking Sheriff Hawkins' path.

Sheriff Hawkins spread his legs wide in best gunfighter fashion, like he'd seen in a picture of Wild Bill Hickcock.

Sheriff hawkins spat his words. "My mind' made up, Powers. This town's too small for two lawmen. So I'm killin' you off!"

"You don't say!"

Sheriff Hawkins spoke over his shoulder. "Spread out, men. One of these white or black-dressed sonsofbitches grab, you pull faster, savvy?"

He got no reply.

"Who you talkin' to?" Mel Powers asked.

Sheriff Hawkins whirled, hand splayed over holster. He stared behind him. He saw no humans, for they were in hiding, afraid of stray bullets.

His face paled.

He turned and faced Powers and the gun-hung twins. Each bore a wide, and happy, grin.

They had him corraled. He'd not kill them. They'd kill him. And Sheriff Hawkins turned and fled.

He started down-street. He heard guns roaring behind. He heard the shouts and hooting of the Half Circle V men. He almost ran into the town flagpole.

The flagpole was around forty feet tall. It was an overlength telephone pole old man Powers had bought when the railroad put through its telegraph line, many miles away.

Powers had had it freighted to Mad Horse and implanted in the street's middle. It had no pulley or rope. To hang out the flag each national holiday it had to be climbed.

Therefore climbing-spikes had been driven into its creosoted length the proper distance apart.

Sheriff Hawkins grabbed a spike. He scrambled upward. Bullets ripped splinters over his head, under his boots. He stopped halfway up and stared down, a queer-looking object—more monkey than human—his green smeared by black creosote.

He glanced down at his gun. It still rode in holster.

He stared down at Mel Powers who ordered the

twins, "Don't shoot any more at him! From now on, he's my meat!"

The twins began reloading.

Sheriff Hawkins glanced toward the saloon. He saw his mother come on the run. She carried her sawed-off shotgun.

Cal Sherman ran abreast of his mother. Cal carried no weapon but he had his pistol on his hip.

Old One Step hobbled madly behind. He carried his old pistol. He was hollering something to Mickie O'Hannigan.

Sheriff Hawkins could not hear what One Step hollered. There was too much buzzing in his ears. His throat was bone-dry.

An aura came over his eyes. He felt his muscles begin to lose strength. He thought for one terrible moment he'd fall from the pole.

By sheer effort, he fought off blackness. Finally his mother's words came to him.

"Don't shoot, son. If you don't shoot, they dare not shoot you! But if you shot one of them—first—"

One Step caught his mother's arms. He plainly wanted her shotgun. His mother planted her feet wide.

One Step said, "Give me that shotgun, woman. They might jus' be treein' him, not aimin' to kill him! An' this ain't no place for a woman, anyway!"

"God damn you, One Step!"

"Please, Miss O'Hannigan," Cal Sherman said. "Let him an' me handle this, I pray you!"

"He's right, Mickie," a woman's voice said.

Mary Malone had arrived. She'd been in her room doing some ironing. She wore a dressing-gown and houseslippers.

Powers had stopped shooting. He and Ted watched

the oncomers—Mickie, One Step, Mary and Cal. "You watch the flagpole, Max," Powers ordered. "He make a move to come down, blister his soles!"

"Okay, boss."

Sheriff Hawkins had twisted around, back now to the pole, boots braced solidly on the climbing-spikes. He stared down. He looked like a huge green frog suspended in space.

Mickie spoke to Cal. "This is no business of yours, Cal."

Cal Sherman shook his head. "Maybe no, maybe yes, Miss O'Hannigan. But Powers ordered me out of town, remember?"

"That doesn't call for you with us. It's your safety I think of, Cal."

Cal pulled in Montana air. "I thank you for your kind feelings, Miss O'Hannigan. But I aim to stay in your town. I like you and I like the people—except for a few, of course. And if I don't go, sooner or later Powers and I will clash, so why not now?"

"Well said," One Step assured.

Mickie gave One Step the shotgun. "If they shoot an' kill him—"

"I'll shoot an' kill them," One Step said.

The four started forward again. Then it was that at that moment the second element came into view at the south end of Main Street.

"The farmers," One Step said.

The hoemen came in a body. Some were astraddle mules and horses, others walked, others rode buggies and spring-wagons and democrats. Many women and older children were in the group. And all were armed with rifles or shotguns or pistols.

Big Sig Nelson headed them, leading a horse packing an empty saddle.

One Step peered. "That's Mike Western's horse he's leadin'," he said.

Now all eyes—except Max's—were on the approaching farmers. Max watched Sheriff Hawkins on the telephone pole. Max had been given orders to watch Sheriff Hawkins. Max always obeyed his superior's orders.

"They've finally busted loose," One Step said.

Cal scowled. "Why are they leading Western's horse. And why an empty saddle?"

"Maybe they just found the horse," Mary Malone said.

Another woman said, "That could be so."

Bea Graham had just moved in, sunlight dancing from her glorious red hair.

"Where do you suppose Western is?" Cal asked.

"Across the street," Mickie said.

A man had emerged from the space between the barber shop and the former newspaper office.

Cal immediately recognized Mike Western. Western had his golden collie with him. Western looked like he'd just stepped out of the jaws of hell.

He was unshaven. His face was a mass of scabs. Now he fell to one knee, rifle rising to cover Mel Powers, who had his back to the farmer.

Western's scream knifed the air. "Turn aroun' an' face me, Powers!"

Powers whirled, Ted whirled—but Max still kept watching Sheriff Hawkins. Western said, "You dirty sonsofbitches— You double-crossed me, you almost killed me with them ropes—"

Mel Powers shot at Western. Western took the lead in his chest. Western shot as he fell forward.

His bullet didn't hit Mel Powers. It hit Max in the heart. Max dropped in his boots.

Western laughed with maniacal glee. "I got me one of the sonsofbitches—Now I'll get me another!"

He raised his arms. He was again going to shoot. There was one thing wrong, though—his arms held no rifle.

He'd dropped his Winchester. For one wild second Western stared about, searching for a rifle he couldn't see. He fell to all fours. From somewhere he found new strength.

He scrambled back between the two buildings with bullets ripping splinters around him, for now both Ted and Powers were shooting.

Western disappeared.

Western's terrified collie leaped into the street. Powers swung his smoking six-gun on the running dog. Powers shot just once.

The collie went end over end, dust flying. He didn't get up.

"The dirty bastard," Cal said. "He shot that dog just to kill something, the sonofabitch!"

Then it was that poised Sheriff Hawkins screamed, "I'm a bird! I just got out of my cage! I'm free at last!"

His scream jerked all eyes upward. White-clad Powers was directly below the pseudo sheriff, black-garbed Ted at Powers' right.

"Stay where you are, son!" Mickie hollered.

Sheriff Hawkins spoke to Mickie O'Hannigan. "I thank you, mama, for what you have done for me."

And then, he leaped forward.

He lanced his young, tough body into space. He fell like a green-colored comet.

Mel Powers leaped backwards too late. Sheriff Hawkins landed directly on Powers.

Hawkins and Powers crashed to the planks. Ted

leaped back, gun rising. He was puzzled. He couldn't shoot Sheriff Hawkins without hitting Mel Powers.

Ted circled Powers and Hawkins, gun pointing down, looking for a chance to shoot Hawkins and miss his boss.

"You shoot that boy," Cal Sherman said, "and I'm killing you, you black-coated bastard!"

Mickie hollered, "My boy's gun is loaded with blanks!"

But Mickie had erred. Sheriff Hank Hawkins' six-shooter now packed real cartridges. Green clashed with white there on the plank sidewalk, and out of the tangle came roar and flame.

Cal dimly remembered counting three shots.

Then, it was over.

Mel Powers lay motionless on his back. A bullet had hit him between the eyes, breaking the bridge of his nose.

Sheriff Hawkins looked wildly about. He was on his knees. He tried to get to his boots. His green was covered with blood. Powers' snow white was no longer white. It was red.

Sheriff Hawkins went back to his knees. He stared wide-eyed at his mother who hurried toward him. He opened his mouth. No words came. Then he lay gently on his side, mouth open, and Cal saw his eyes begin to glass over.

Then, Ted made his play.

Ted was completely mystified. Things had happened too fast for his severely-limited intelligence. He stared at unmoving Mel Powers. His eyes went beyond his boss. They landed on his brother.

Max, his twin— His life-long friend— Max was dead, now—and he, Ted, was alone.

Ted threw back his head. He heard rifles and shotguns and pistols hammering down-street. Farmers were shooting it out with the other Half Circle V gunmen. They were having a gunfight.

Ted cupped hands to his mouth. "The boss is dead," he screamed. "He can pay us no more—"

"I'm pullin' out," a gunman screeched.

The gunmen broke ranks. They ran between buildings, fight forgotten. They had horses tied there. They hit saddles and loped out fast, whipping their broncs down the hind-legs.

Ted turned about. His eyes landed on Cal Sherman. "You driftin' sonofabitch!" Ted told Cal. "Mel ordered you to leave! You're still here! I'll plant you here permanently!"

Cal still had his weapon in holster. They told him afterwards what happened. He went fast to his right. Ted shot and missed. Cal was on his belly on the ground. He had his six-shooter out in front of him.

Cal shot second.

Ted took the bullet in his throat. He stood for a moment, staring at nothing. His gun dropped. Then he came over the smoking weapon, there in the liquid dust of old Montana.

He fell on his front. His nose and mouth buried themselves in the dust. He didn't move again. Wind gently ruffled his black shirt.

Cal got shakily to his boots. Automatically, he reloaded his six-shooter aware that it was all over. He looked south toward the farmers. They were coming his direction. Two supported a wounded man between them. It reminded Cal of San Juan Hill. His blood went cold.

His weapon reloaded, he holstered it. He looked at

Mickie who knelt beside her dead son.

She won't have to take him to Warm Springs now, Cal thought.

His knees were weak. He walked across the planks and leaned against a building. The shade was cool.

Farmer Newbarger came up. "Western just died. He had some words to say about thet shootin' out in the south foothills."

Cal Sherman's heart leaped.

"Western was supposed to beat up on Graham that mornin'. Powers ordered him to. But Mike got drunk and went to sleep in the hotel and overslept and didn't ride out to that south clearing."

"Why are you telling me this?" Cal's voice sounded dim, faraway, in his own ears.

"Western said he had no idea what had happened out there."

Cal Sherman had. The Half Circle V men had evidently figured Graham had killed Western before Graham had ridden into that clearing. So they had killed Graham in cold-blood.

That added up.

Relief flooded Cal Sherman. Only he would know what had transpired out there on that southern clearing. And the secret would go to the grave with him.

"Us farmers got a plan, Mr. Sherman."

"What is it, Mr. Newbarger?"

"This range has no law. There has to be somebody to hold the law-badge or men will run rampant, they're still that uncivilized. I've been appointed a committee of one to ask you to temporarily take over as lawman."

"I shall be happy to oblige, sir."

"We thank you, Mr. Sherman."

The farmer left and Mary said, "I'll ride to the

railroad wire. The dog soldiers will move in and maintain law and order until a proper election can be held."

"Good idea," Cal said.

Mickie O'Hannigan had taken over. She was engineering the carrying of the dead to the small building used as morgue. Soon six others would follow Sheriff Ike Monday to the town graveyard.

Cal looked about. He leaned against the former press-shop.

"You folks don't know much about me," he said. "I just came out of the war. I used to be reporter and printer for Captain Bucky O'Neill on his newspaper, *Hoofs and Horns,* down in Prescott, Arizona Territory—my home range."

"And you want to start a newspaper here," Mary Malone said.

"How'd you guess?" Cal asked.

Bea answered with, "Why would you waste so much time looking at the press inside this building if you didn't want to use it?"

Cal said, "I can't hide anything from you two . . ."

He looked down at them. A redhead, smart as a buggy-whipper snapper, and a dark-haired beautiful woman, sharp with cards and nice to look at. *This will be interesting,* he told himself, *very, very interesting* . . .

"Let's get to work," Cal Sherman said.

"Doing what?" Bea asked.

Mary smiled. "Ripping boards off windows, of course."

Rusty nails screeched.